P9-BYJ-644

ON CHESIL BEACH

ALSO BY IAN McEWAN

First Love, Last Rites
In Between the Sheets
The Cement Garden
The Comfort of Strangers
The Child in Time
The Innocent
Black Dogs
The Daydreamer
Enduring Love
Amsterdam
Atonement
Saturday

ON CHESIL BEACH

IAN McEWAN

NAN A. TALESE
DOUBLEDAY
New York London Toronto
Sydney Auckland

PUBLISHED BY NAN A. TALESE
AN IMPRINT OF DOUBLEDAY

Copyright © 2007 by Ian McEwan

All Rights Reserved

First published in Great Britain in 2007 by Jonathan Cape.

Published in the United States by Nan A. Talese, an imprint of The Doubleday Broadway Publishing Group, a division of Random House, Inc., New York.
www.nantalese.com

DOUBLEDAY is a registered trademark of Random House, Inc.

This book is a work of fiction. Names, characters, businesses, organizations, places, events, and incidents either are the product of the author's imagination or are used fictitiously. Any resemblance to actual persons, living or dead, events, or locales is entirely coincidental.

Book design by Marysarah Quinn
Title page illustration by Louis Jones

Library of Congress Cataloging-in-Publication Data
McEwan, Ian.
On Chesil Beach / Ian McEwan.
p. cm.
I. Title.
PR6063.C4O6 2007
823'.914—dc22 2006100720

ISBN 978-0-385-52240-3

PRINTED IN THE UNITED STATES OF AMERICA

First U.S. Edition

10 9 8 7 6 5 4 3 2 1

To Annalena

ON CHESIL BEACH

ONE

They were young, educated, and both virgins on this, their wedding night, and they lived in a time when a conversation about sexual difficulties was plainly impossible. But it is never easy. They had just sat down to supper in a tiny sitting room on the first floor of a Georgian inn. In the next room, visible through the open door, was a four-poster bed, rather narrow, whose bedcover was pure white and stretched startlingly smooth, as though by no human hand. Edward did not mention that he had never stayed in a hotel before, whereas Florence, after many trips as a child with her father, was an old hand. Superficially, they were in fine spirits. Their wedding, at St. Mary's, Oxford, had gone well; the service was decorous, the reception jolly, the send-off from school and college friends raucous and uplifting. Her parents had not condescended to his, as they had feared, and his mother had not significantly misbehaved, or completely forgotten the purpose of the occasion. The couple had driven away in a small car belonging to Florence's mother and arrived in the early evening at their hotel on the Dorset coast in weather that was not perfect for mid-July or the circumstances, but entirely adequate: it was not raining, but nor was it quite warm enough, according to Florence, to eat outside on the terrace as they had hoped. Edward thought it was, but, polite to a fault, he would not think of contradicting her on such an evening.

So they were eating in their rooms before the partially open French windows that gave onto a balcony and a view of a portion of the English Channel, and Chesil Beach with its infinite shingle. Two youths in dinner jackets served them from a trolley parked outside in the corridor, and their comings and goings through what was generally known as the honeymoon suite made the waxed oak boards squeak comically against the silence. Proud and protective, the young man watched closely for any gesture or expression that might have seemed satirical. He could not have tolerated any sniggering. But these lads from a nearby village went about their business with bowed backs and closed faces, and their manner was tentative, their hands shook as they set items down on the starched linen tablecloth. They were nervous too.

This was not a good moment in the history of English cuisine, but no one much minded at the time, except visitors from abroad. The formal meal began, as so many did then, with a slice of melon decorated by a single glazed cherry. Out in the corridor, in silver dishes on candle-heated plate warmers, waited slices of long-ago roasted beef in a thickened gravy, soft boiled vegetables, and potatoes of a bluish hue. The wine was from France, though no particular region was mentioned on the label, which was embellished with a solitary darting swallow. It would not have crossed Edward's mind to have ordered a red.

Desperate for the waiters to leave, he and Florence turned in their chairs to consider the view of a broad mossy lawn, and beyond, a tangle of flowering shrubs and trees clinging to a steep bank that descended to a lane that led to the beach. They could see the beginnings of a footpath, dropping by muddy steps, a way lined by weeds of extravagant size—giant rhubarb and cabbages they looked like, with swollen stalks more than six feet tall, bending under the weight of dark, thick-veined leaves. The garden vegetation rose up, sensuous and tropical in its profusion, an effect heightened by the gray, soft light and a delicate mist drifting in from the sea, whose steady motion of advance and withdrawal made sounds of gentle thunder, then sudden hissing against the pebbles. Their plan was to change into rough shoes after supper and walk on the shingle between the sea and the lagoon known as the fleet, and if they had not finished the wine, they would take that along, and swig from the bottle like gentlemen of the road.

And they had so many plans, giddy plans, heaped up before them in the misty future, as richly tangled as the summer flora of the Dorset coast, and as beautiful. Where and how they would live, who their close friends would be, his job with her father's firm, her musical career and what to do with the money her father had given her, and how they would not be like other people, at least, not inwardly. This was still the era—it would end later in that famous decade—when to be young was a social encumbrance, a mark of irrelevance, a faintly embarrassing condition for which marriage was the beginning of a cure. Almost strangers, they stood, strangely together, on a new pinnacle of existence, gleeful that their new status promised to promote them out of their endless youth—Edward and Florence, free at last! One of their favorite topics was their childhoods, not so much the pleasures as the fog of comical misconceptions from which they had emerged, and the various parental errors and outdated practices they could now forgive.

From these new heights they could see clearly, but they could not describe to each other certain contradictory feelings: they separately worried about the moment, sometime soon after dinner, when their new maturity would be tested, when they would lie down together on the four-poster bed and reveal themselves fully to each other. For over a year, Edward had been mesmerized by the prospect that on the evening of a given date in July the most sensitive portion of himself would reside, however briefly, within a naturally formed cavity inside this cheerful, pretty, formidably intelligent woman. How this was to be achieved without absurdity, or disappointment, troubled him. His specific worry, based on one unfortunate experience, was of overexcitement, of what he had heard someone describe as "arriving too soon." The matter was rarely out of his thoughts, but though his fear of failure was great, his eagerness—for rapture, for resolution—was far greater.

Florence's anxieties were more serious, and there were moments during the journey from Oxford when she thought she was about to draw on all her courage to speak her mind. But what troubled her was unutterable, and she could barely frame it for herself. Where he merely suffered conventional first-night nerves, she experienced a visceral dread, a helpless disgust as palpable as seasickness. For much of the time, through all the months of merry wedding preparation, she managed to ignore this stain on her happiness, but whenever her thoughts turned toward a close embrace—she preferred no other term—her stomach tightened dryly, she was nauseous at the back of her throat. In a modern, forward-looking handbook that was supposed to be helpful to young brides, with its cheery tones and exclamation marks and numbered illustrations, she came across certain phrases or words that almost made her gag: *mucous membrane*, and the sinister and glistening *glans*. Other phrases offended her intelligence, particularly those concerning entrances: *Not long before he enters her* . . . or, *now at last he enters her*, and, *happily, soon after he has entered her* . . . Was she obliged on the night to transform herself for Edward into a kind of portal or drawing room through which he might process? Almost as frequent was a word that suggested to her nothing but pain, flesh parted before a knife: *penetration.*

In optimistic moments she tried to convince herself that she suffered no more than a heightened form of squeamishness, which was bound to pass. Certainly, the thought of Edward's testicles, pendulous below his *engorged* penis—another horrifying term—had the potency to make her upper lip curl, and the idea of herself being touched "down there" by someone else, even someone she loved, was as repulsive as, say, a surgical procedure on her eye. But her squeamishness did not extend to babies. She liked them; she had looked after her cousin's little boys on occasion and enjoyed herself. She thought she would love being pregnant by Edward, and in the abstract, at least, she had no fears about childbirth. If only she could, like the mother of Jesus, arrive at that swollen state by magic.

Florence suspected that there was something profoundly wrong with her, that she had always been different, and that at last she was about to be exposed. Her problem, she thought, was greater, deeper, than straightforward physical disgust; her whole being was in revolt against a prospect of entanglement and flesh; her composure and essential happiness were about to be violated. She simply did not want to be "entered" or "penetrated." Sex with Edward could not be the summation of her joy, but was the price she must pay for it.

She knew she should have spoken up long ago, as soon as he proposed, long before the visit to the sincere and soft-voiced vicar, and dinners with their respective parents, before the wedding guests were invited, the gift list devised and lodged with a department store, and the marquee and photographer hired, and all the other irreversible arrangements. But what could she have said, what possible terms could she have used when she could not have named the matter to herself? And she loved Edward, not with the hot, moist passion she had read about, but warmly, deeply, sometimes like a daughter, sometimes almost maternally. She loved cuddling him, and having his enormous arm around her shoulders, and being kissed by him, though she disliked his tongue in her mouth and had wordlessly made this clear. She thought he was original, unlike anyone she had ever met. He always had a paperback book, usually history, in his jacket pocket in case he found himself in a queue or a waiting room. He marked what he read with a pencil stub. He was virtually the only man Florence had met who did not smoke. None of his socks matched.

He had only one tie, narrow, knitted, dark blue, which he wore nearly all the time with a white shirt. She adored his curious mind, his mild country accent, the huge strength in his hands, the unpredictable swerves and drifts of his conversation, his kindness to her, and the way his soft brown eyes, resting on her when she spoke, made her feel enveloped in a friendly cloud of love. At the age of twenty-two, she had no doubt that she wanted to spend the rest of her life with Edward Mayhew. How could she have dared risk losing him?

There was no one she could have talked to. Ruth, her sister, was too young, and her mother, perfectly wonderful in her way, was too intellectual, too brittle, an old-fashioned bluestocking. Whenever she confronted an intimate problem, she tended to adopt the public manner of the lecture hall, and use longer and longer words, and make references to books she thought everyone should have read. Only when the matter was safely bundled up in this way might she sometimes relax into kindliness, though that was rare, and even then you had no idea what advice you were receiving. Florence had some terrific friends from school and music college who posed the opposite problem: they adored intimate talk and reveled in each other's problems. They all knew each other, and were too eager with their phone calls and letters. She could not trust them with a secret, nor did she blame them, for she was part of the group. She would not have trusted herself. She was alone with a problem she did not know how to begin to address, and all she had in the way of wisdom was her paperback guide. On its garish red covers were portrayed two smiling bug-eyed matchstick figures holding hands, drawn clumsily in white chalk, as though by an innocent child.

They ate the melon in less than two minutes while the lads, instead of waiting out in the corridor, stood well back, near the door, fingering their bow ties and tight collars and fiddling with their cuffs. Their blank expressions did not change as they observed Edward offer Florence, with an ironic flourish, his glazed cherry. Playfully, she sucked it from his fingers and held his gaze as she deliberately chewed, letting him see her tongue, conscious that in flirting with him like this she would be making matters worse for herself. She should not start what she could not sustain, but pleasing him in any way she could was helpful: it made her feel less than entirely useless. If only eating a sticky cherry was all that was required.

To show that he was not troubled by the presence of the waiters, though he longed for them to leave, Edward smiled as he sat back with his wine and called over his shoulder, "Any more of those things?"

"Ain't none, sir. Sorry sir."

But the hand that held the wineglass trembled as he struggled to contain his sudden happiness, his exaltation. She appeared to glow before him, and she was lovely—beautiful, sensuous, gifted, good-natured beyond belief.

The boy who had spoken nipped forward to clear away. His colleague was just outside the room, transferring the second course, the roast, to their plates. It was not possible to wheel the trolley into the honeymoon suite for the proper silver service on account of a two-step difference in level between it and the corridor, a consequence of poor planning when the Elizabethan farmhouse was "Georgianized" in the mid-eighteenth century.

The couple were briefly alone, though they heard the scrape of spoons over dishes, and the lads murmuring by the open door. Edward laid his hand over Florence's and said, for the hundredth time that day, in a whisper, "I love you," and she said it straight back, and she truly meant it.

Edward had a degree, a first in history from University College, London. In three short years he studied wars, rebellions, famines, pestilences, the rise and collapse of empires, revolutions that consumed their children, agricultural hardship, industrial squalor, the cruelty of ruling elites—a colorful pageant of oppression, misery and failed hopes. He understood how constrained and meager lives could be, generation after generation. In the grand view of things, these peaceful, prosperous times England was experiencing now were rare, and within them his and Florence's joy was exceptional, even unique. In his final year he had made a special study of the "great man" theory of history—was it really outmoded to believe that forceful individuals could shape national destiny? Certainly his tutor thought so: in his view History, properly capitalized, was driven forward by ineluctable forces toward inevitable, necessary ends, and soon the subject would be understood as a science. But the lives Edward examined in detail—Caesar, Charlemagne, Frederick the Second, Catherine the Great, Nelson and Napoleon (Stalin he dropped, at his tutor's insistence)—rather suggested the contrary. A ruthless personality, naked opportunism and luck, Edward had argued, could divert the fates of millions, a wayward conclusion that earned him a B minus, almost imperiling his first.

An incidental discovery was that even legendary success brought little happiness, only redoubled restlessness, gnawing ambition. As he dressed for the wedding that morning (tails, top hat, a thorough drenching in cologne), he had decided that none of the figures on his list could have known his kind of satisfaction. His elation was a form of greatness in itself. Here he was, a gloriously fulfilled, or almost fulfilled, man. At the age of twenty-two, he had already outshone them all.

He was gazing at his wife now, into her intricately flecked hazel eyes, into those pure whites touched by a bloom of the faintest milky blue. The lashes were thick and dark, like a child's, and there was something childlike too in the solemnity of her face at rest. It was a lovely face, with a sculpted look that in a certain light brought to mind an American Indian woman, a high-born squaw. She had a strong jaw, and her smile was broad and artless, right into the creases at the corners of her eyes. She was big-boned—certain matrons at the wedding knowingly remarked on her generous hips. Her breasts, which Edward had touched and even kissed, though nowhere near enough, were small. Her violinist's hands were pale and powerful, her long arms likewise; at her school sports days she had been adept at throwing the javelin.

Edward had never cared for classical music, but now he was learning its sprightly argot—*legato, pizzicato, con brio.* Slowly, through brute repetition, he was coming to recognize and even like certain pieces. There was one she played with her friends that especially moved him. When she practiced her scales and arpeggios at home she wore a headband, an endearing touch that caused him to dream about the daughter they might have one day. Florence's playing was sinuous and exact, and she was known for the richness of her tone. One tutor said he had never encountered a student who made an open string sing so warmly. When she was before the music stand in the rehearsal room in London, or in her room at her parents' house in Oxford, with Edward sprawled on the bed, watching and desiring her, she held herself gracefully, with back straight and head lifted proudly, and read the music with a commanding, almost haughty expression that stirred him. That look had such certitude, such knowledge of the path to pleasure.

When the business was music, she was always confident and fluid in her movements—rosining a bow, restringing her instrument, rearranging the room to accommodate her three friends from college for the string quartet that was her passion. She was the undisputed leader, and always had the final word in their many musical disagreements. But in the rest of her life she was surprisingly clumsy and unsure, forever stubbing a toe or knocking things over or bumping her head. The fingers that could manage the double stopping in a Bach partita were just as clever at spilling a full teacup over a linen tablecloth or dropping a glass onto a stone floor. She would trip over her feet if she thought she was being watched—she confided to Edward that she found it an ordeal to be in the street, walking toward a friend from a distance. And whenever she was anxious or too self-conscious, her hand would rise repeatedly to her forehead to brush away an imaginary strand of hair, a gentle, fluttering motion that would continue long after the source of stress had vanished.

How could he fail to love someone so strangely and warmly particular, so painfully honest and self-aware, whose every thought and emotion appeared naked to view, streaming like charged particles through her changing expressions and gestures? Even without her strong-boned beauty he would have had to love her. And she loved him with such intensity, such excruciating physical reticence. Not only his passions, heightened by the lack of a proper outlet, but also his protective instincts were aroused. But was she really so vulnerable? He had peeped once into her school report folder and seen her intelligence-tests results: one hundred and fifty-two, seventeen points above his own score. This was an age when these quotients were held to measure something as tangible as height or weight. When he sat in on a rehearsal with the quartet, and she had a difference of opinion on a phrasing or tempo or dynamic with Charles, the chubby and assertive cellist, whose face shone with late-flowering acne, Edward was intrigued by how cool Florence could be. She did not argue, she listened calmly, then announced her decision. No sign then of the little hair-brushing action. She knew her stuff, and she was determined to lead, the way the first violin should. She seemed to be able to get her rather frightening father to do what she wanted. Many months before the wedding he had, at her suggestion, offered Edward a job. Whether he really wanted it, or dared refuse it, was another matter. And she knew, by some womanly osmosis, exactly what was needed at that celebration, from the size of marquee to the quantity of summer pudding, and just how much it was reasonable to expect her father to pay.

"Here it comes," she whispered as she squeezed his hand, warning him off another sudden intimacy. The waiters were arriving with their plates of beef, his piled twice the height of hers. They also brought sherry trifle and cheddar cheese and mint chocolates, which they arranged on a sideboard. After mumbling advice about the summoning bell by the fireplace—it must be pressed hard and held down—the lads withdrew, closing the door behind them with immense care. Then came a tinkling of the trolley retreating down the corridor, then, after a silence, a whoop or a hoot that could easily have come from the hotel bar downstairs, and at last, the newlyweds were properly alone.

A shift or a strengthening of the wind brought them the sound of waves breaking, like a distant shattering of glasses. The mist was lifting to reveal in part the contours of the low hills, curving away above the shoreline to the east. They could see a luminous gray smoothness that may have been the silky surface of the sea itself, or the lagoon, or the sky—it was difficult to tell. The altered breeze carried through the parted French windows an enticement, a salty scent of oxygen and open space that seemed at odds with the starched table linen, the cornflour-stiffened gravy, and the heavy polished silver they were taking in their hands. The wedding lunch had been huge and prolonged. They were not hungry. It was in theory open to them to abandon their plates, seize the wine bottle by the neck and run down to the shore and kick their shoes off and exult in their liberty. There was no one in the hotel who would have wanted to stop them. They were adults at last, on holiday, free to do as they chose. In just a few years' time, that would be the kind of thing quite ordinary young people would do. But for now, the times held them. Even when Edward and Florence were alone, a thousand unacknowledged rules still applied. It was precisely because they were adults that they did not do childish things like walk away from a meal that others had taken pains to prepare. It was dinnertime, after all. And being childlike was not yet honorable, or in fashion.

Still, Edward was troubled by the call of the beach, and if he had known how to propose it, or justify it, he might have suggested going out straightaway. He had read aloud to Florence from a guidebook that said that thousands of years of pounding storms had sifted and graded the size of pebbles along the eighteen miles of beach, with the bigger stones at the eastern end. The legend was that local fishermen landing at night knew exactly where they were by the grade of shingle. Florence had suggested they might see for themselves by comparing handfuls gathered a mile apart. Trudging along the beach would have been better than sitting here. The ceiling, low enough already, appeared nearer to his head, and closing in. Rising from his plate, mingling with the sea breeze, was a clammy odor, like the breath of the family dog. Perhaps he was not quite as joyous as he kept telling himself he was. He felt a terrible pressure narrowing his thoughts, constraining his speech, and he was in acute physical discomfort—his trousers or underwear seemed to have shrunk.

So if a genie had appeared at their table to grant Edward's most urgent request, he would not have asked for any beach in the world. All he wanted, all he could think of, was himself and Florence lying naked together on or in the bed next door, confronting at last that awesome experience that seemed as remote from daily life as a vision of religious ecstasy, or even death itself. The prospect—was it actually going to happen? to him?—once more sent cool fingers through his lower gut, and he caught himself in a momentary swooning motion which he concealed behind a contented sigh.

Like most young men of his time, or any time, without an easy manner, or means to sexual expression, he indulged constantly in what one enlightened authority was now calling "self-pleasuring." Edward was pleased to discover the term. He was born too late in the century, in 1940, to believe that he was abusing his body, that his sight would be impaired, or that God watched on with stern incredulity as he bent daily to the task. Or even that everyone knew about it from his pale and inward look. All the same, a certain ill-defined disgrace hung over his efforts, a sense of failure and waste and, of course, loneliness. And pleasure was really an incidental benefit. The goal was release—from urgent, thought-confining desire for what could not be immediately had. How extraordinary it was, that a self-made spoonful, leaping clear of his body, should instantly free his mind to confront afresh Nelson's decisiveness at Aboukir Bay.

Edward's single most important contribution to the wedding arrangements was to refrain, for over a week. Not since he was twelve had he been so entirely chaste with himself. He wanted to be in top form for his bride. It was not easy, especially at night in bed, or in the mornings as he woke, or in the long afternoons, or in the hours before lunch, or after supper, during the hours before bed. Now here they were at last, married and alone. Why did he not rise from his roast, cover her in kisses and lead her toward the four-poster next door? It was not so simple. He had a fairly long history of engaging with Florence's shyness. He had come to respect it, even revere it, mistaking it for a form of coyness, a conventional veil for a richly sexual nature. In all, part of the intricate depth of her personality, and proof of her quality. He persuaded himself that he preferred her this way. He did not spell it out for himself, but her reticence suited his own ignorance and lack of confidence; a more sensual and demanding woman, a *wild* woman, might have terrified him.

Their courtship had been a pavane, a stately unfolding, bound by protocols never agreed or voiced but generally observed. Nothing was ever discussed—nor did they feel the lack of intimate talk. These were matters beyond words, beyond definition. The language and practice of therapy, the currency of feelings diligently shared, mutually analyzed, were not yet in general circulation. While one heard of wealthier people going in for psychoanalysis, it was not yet customary to regard oneself in everyday terms as an enigma, as an exercise in narrative history, or as a problem waiting to be solved.

Between Edward and Florence, nothing happened quickly. Important advances, permissions wordlessly granted to extend what he was allowed to see or caress, were attained only gradually. The day in October he first saw her naked breasts long preceded the day he could touch them—December 19. He kissed them in February, though not her nipples, which he grazed with his lips once, in May. She allowed herself to advance across his own body with even greater caution. Sudden moves or radical suggestions on his part could undo months of good work. The evening in the cinema at a showing of *A Taste of Honey* when he took her hand and plunged it between his legs set the process back weeks. She became, not frosty, or even cool—that was never her way—but imperceptibly remote, perhaps disappointed, or even faintly betrayed. She retreated from him somehow without letting him ever feel in doubt about her love. Then at last they were back on course: when they were alone one Saturday afternoon in late March, with the rain falling heavily outside the windows of the disorderly sitting room of his parents' tiny house in the Chiltern Hills, she let her hand rest briefly on, or near, his penis. For less than fifteen seconds, in rising hope and ecstasy, he felt her through two layers of fabric. As soon as she pulled away he knew he could bear it no more. He asked her to marry him.

He could not have known what it cost her to put a hand—it was the back of her hand—in such a place. She loved him, she wanted to please him, but she had to overcome considerable distaste. It was an honest attempt—she may have been clever, but she was without guile. She kept that hand in place for as long as she could, until she felt a stirring and hardening beneath the gray flannel of his trousers. She experienced a living thing, quite separate from her Edward—and she recoiled. Then he blurted out his proposal, and in the rush of emotion, the delight and hilarity and relief, the sudden embraces, she momentarily forgot her little shock. And he was so astonished by his own decisiveness, as well as mentally cramped by unresolved desire, that he could have had little idea of the contradiction she began to live with from that day on, the secret affair between disgust and joy.

• • •

They were alone then, and theoretically free to do whatever they wanted, but they went on eating the dinner they had no appetite for. Florence set down her knife and reached for Edward's hand and squeezed. From downstairs they heard the wireless, the chimes of Big Ben at the start of the ten o'clock news. Along this stretch of coast television reception was poor because of the hills just inland. The older guests would be down there in the sitting room, taking the measure of the world with their nightcaps—the hotel had a good selection of single malts—and some of the men would be filling their pipes for one last time that day. Gathering around the wireless for the main bulletin was a wartime habit they would never break. Edward and Florence heard the muffled headlines and caught the name of the prime minister, and then a minute or two later his familiar voice raised in a speech. Harold Macmillan had been addressing a conference in Washington about the arms race and the need for a test-ban treaty. Who could disagree that it was folly to go on testing H-bombs in the atmosphere and irradiating the whole planet? But no one under thirty—certainly not Edward and Florence—believed a British prime minister held much sway in global affairs. Every year the empire shrank as another few countries took their rightful independence. Now there was almost nothing left, and the world belonged to the Americans and the Russians. Britain, England, was a minor power—saying this gave a certain blasphemous pleasure. Downstairs, of course, they took a different view. Anyone over forty would have fought or suffered in the war and known death on an unusual scale, and would not have been able to believe that a drift into irrelevance was the reward for all the sacrifice.

Edward and Florence would be voting for the first time in the next general election and were keen on the idea of a Labour landslide as great as the famous victory of 1945. In a year or two, the older generation that still dreamed of empire must surely give way to politicians like Gaitskell, Wilson, Crosland—new men with a vision of a modern country where there was equality and things actually got done. If America could have an exuberant and handsome President Kennedy, then Britain could have something similar—at least in spirit, for there was no one quite so glamorous in the Labour Party. The Blimps, still fighting the last war, still nostalgic for its discipline and privations—their time was up. Edward and Florence's shared sense that one day soon the country would be transformed for the better, that youthful energies were pushing to escape, like steam under pressure, merged with the excitement of their own adventure together. The sixties was their first decade of adult life, and it surely belonged to them. The pipe smokers downstairs in their silver-buttoned blazers, with their double measures of Caol Ila and memories of campaigns in North Africa and Normandy and their cultivated remnants of army slang—they could have no claim on the future. Time, gentlemen, please!

The rising mist continued to unveil the nearby trees, the bare green cliffs behind the lagoon and portions of a silver sea, and the smooth evening air poured in around the table, and they continued their pretense of eating, trapped in the moment by private anxieties. Florence was merely moving the food around her plate. Edward ate only token morsels of potato, which he carved with the edge of his fork. They listened helplessly to the second item of news, aware of how dull it was of them to be linking their attention to that of the guests downstairs. Their wedding night, and they had nothing to say. The indistinct words rose from under their feet, but they made out "Berlin" and knew instantly that this was the story that lately had captivated everyone. It was an escape from the Communist east to the west of the city by way of a commandeered steamship on the Wannsee, the refugees cowering by the wheelhouse to dodge the bullets of the East German guards. They listened to that, and now, intolerably, the third item, the concluding session of an Islamic conference in Baghdad.

Bound to world events by their own stupidity! It could not go on. It was time to act. Edward loosened his tie and firmly set down his knife and fork in parallel on his plate.

"We could go downstairs and listen properly."

He hoped he was being humorous, directing his sarcasm against them both, but his words emerged with surprising ferocity, and Florence blushed. She thought he was criticizing her for preferring the wireless to him, and before he could soften or lighten his remark she said hurriedly, "Or we could go and lie on the bed," and nervously swiped an invisible hair from her forehead. To demonstrate how wrong he was, she was proposing what she knew he most wanted and she dreaded. She really would have been happier, or less unhappy, to go down to the lounge and pass the time in quiet conversation with the matrons on the floral-patterned sofas while their men leaned seriously into the news, into the gale of history. Anything but this.

Her husband was smiling and standing and ceremoniously extending his hand across the table. He too was a little pink about the face. His napkin clung to his waist for a moment, hanging absurdly, like a loincloth, and then wafted to the floor in slow motion. There was nothing she could do, beyond fainting, and she was hopeless at acting. She stood and took his hand, certain that her own returning smile was rigidly unconvincing. It would not have helped her to know that Edward in his dreamlike state had never seen her looking lovelier. Something about her arms, he remembered thinking later, slender and vulnerable, and soon to be looped adoringly around his neck. And her beautiful light brown eyes, bright with undeniable passion, and the faint trembling in her lower lip, which even now she wetted with her tongue.

With his free hand he tried to gather up the wine bottle and the half-full glasses, but that was too difficult and distracting—the glasses bulged against each other, causing the stems to cross in his hands and the wine to spill. Instead he seized the bottle alone by the neck. Even in his exalted, jittery condition he thought he understood her customary reticence. All the more cause for joy then, that they faced this momentous occasion, this dividing line of experience, together. And the thrilling fact remained that it was Florence who had suggested lying on the bed. Her changed status had set her free. Still holding her hand, he came around the table and drew near to kiss her.

Believing it was vulgar to do so holding a wine bottle, he set it down again.

"You're very beautiful," he whispered.

She made herself remember how much she loved this man. He was kind, sensitive, he loved her and could do her no harm. She shrugged herself deeper into his embrace, close against his chest, and inhaled his familiar scent, which had a woody quality and was reassuring.

"I'm so happy here with you."

"I'm so happy too," she said quietly.

When they kissed she immediately felt his tongue, tensed and strong, pushing past her teeth, like some bully shouldering his way into a room. Entering her. Her own tongue folded and recoiled in automatic distaste, making even more space for Edward. He knew well enough she did not like this kind of kissing, and he had never before been so assertive. With his lips clamped firmly onto hers, he probed the fleshy floor of her mouth, then moved around inside the teeth of her lower jaw to the empty place where three years ago a wisdom tooth had crookedly grown until removed under general anesthesia. This cavity was where her own tongue usually strayed when she was lost in thought. By association, it was more like an idea than a location, a private, imaginary place rather than a hollow in her gum, and it seemed peculiar to her that another tongue should be able to go there too. It was the hard tapering tip of this alien muscle, quiveringly alive, that repelled her. His left hand was pressed flat above her shoulder blades, just below her neck, levering her head against his. Her claustrophobia and breathlessness grew even as she became more determined that she could not bear to offend him. He was under her tongue, pushing it up against the roof of her mouth, then on top, pushing down, then sliding smoothly along the sides and around, as though he thought he could tie a simple up-and-over knot. He wanted to engage her tongue in some activity of its own, coax it into a hideous mute duet, but she could only shrink and concentrate on not struggling, not gagging, not panicking. If she was sick into his mouth, was one wild thought, their marriage would be instantly over, and she would have to go home and explain herself to her parents. She understood perfectly that this business with tongues, this penetration, was a small-scale enactment, a ritual *tableau vivant*, of what was still to come, like a prologue before an old play that tells you everything that must happen.

As she stood waiting for this particular moment to pass, her hands for form's sake resting on Edward's hips, Florence realized she had stumbled across an empty truth, self-evident enough in retrospect, as primal and ancient as danegeld or droit du seigneur and almost too elemental to define. In deciding to be married, she had agreed to exactly this. She had agreed it was right to do this and have this done to her. When she and Edward and their parents had filed back to the gloomy sacristy after the ceremony to sign the register, it was this they had put their names to, and all the rest—the supposed maturity, the confetti and cake—was a polite distraction. And if she didn't like it, she alone was responsible, for all her choices over the past year were always narrowing to this, and it was all her fault, and now she really did think she was going to be sick.

When he heard her moan, Edward knew that his happiness was almost complete. He had the impression of delightful weightlessness, of standing several inches clear of the ground, so that he towered pleasingly over her. There was pain-pleasure in the way his heart seemed to rise to thud at the base of his throat. He was thrilled by the light touch of her hands, not so very far from his groin, and by the compliance of her lovely body enfolded in his arms and the passionate sound of her breathing rapidly through her nostrils. It brought him to a point of unfamiliar ecstasy, cold and sharp just below the ribs, the way her tongue gently enveloped his as he pushed against it. Perhaps he could persuade her one day soon—perhaps this evening, and she might need no persuading—to take his cock into her soft and beautiful mouth. But that was a thought he needed to scramble away from as fast as he could, for he was in real danger of arriving too soon. He could feel it already beginning, tipping him toward disgrace. Just in time, he thought of the news, of the face of the prime minister, Harold Macmillan, tall, stooping, walruslike, a war hero, an old buffer—he was everything that was not sex, and ideal for the purpose. Trade gap, pay pause, resale price maintenance. Some cursed him for giving away the empire, but there was no choice really, with these winds of change blowing through Africa. No one would have taken that same message from a Labour man. And he had just sacked a third of his cabinet in the "night of the long knives." That took some nerve. Mac the Knife, was one headline, Macbeth! was another. Serious-minded people complained he was burying the nation in an avalanche of TVs, cars, supermarkets and other junk. He let the people have what they wanted. Bread and circuses. A new nation, and now he wanted us to join Europe, and who could say for sure that he was wrong?

Steadied at last. Edward's thoughts dissolved, and he became once more his tongue, the very tip of it, at the same moment that Florence decided she could take no more. She felt pinioned and smothered, she was suffocating, she was nauseous. And she could hear a sound, rising steadily, not in steps like a scale, but in a slow glissando, and not quite a violin or a voice, but somewhere in between, rising and rising unbearably, without ever leaving the audible range, a violin-voice that was just on the edge of making sense, telling her something urgent in sibilants and vowels more primitive than words. It may have been inside the room, or out in the corridor, or only in her ears, like tinnitus. She may even have been making the noise herself. She did not care—she had to get out.

She jerked her head away and pushed free of his arms. Even as he stared at her in surprise, still open-mouthed, a question beginning to form in his expression, she seized his hand and led him toward the bed. It was perverse of her, insane even, when she wanted to run from the room, across the gardens and down the lane, onto the beach to sit alone. Even one minute alone would have helped. But her sense of duty was painfully strong and she could not resist it. She could not bear to let Edward down. And she was convinced she was completely in the wrong. If the entire wedding ensemble of guests and close family had been somehow crammed invisibly into the room to watch, these ghosts would all side with Edward and his urgent, reasonable desires. They would assume there was something wrong with her, and they would be right.

She also knew that her behavior was pitiful. To

survive, to escape one hideous moment, she had to raise the stakes and commit herself to the next, and give the unhelpful impression that she longed for it herself. The final act could not be endlessly deferred. The moment was rising to meet her, just as she was foolishly moving toward it. She was trapped in a game whose rules she could not question. She could not escape the logic that had her leading, or towing, Edward across the room toward the open door of the bedroom and the narrow four-poster bed and its smooth white cover. She had no idea what she would do when they were there, but at least that awful sound had ceased, and in the few seconds it would take to arrive, her mouth and tongue were her own, and she could breathe and try to take possession of herself.

TWO

How did they meet, and why were these lovers in a modern age so timid and innocent? They regarded themselves as too sophisticated to believe in destiny, but still, it remained a paradox to them that so momentous a meeting should have been accidental, so dependent on a hundred minor events and choices. What a terrifying possibility, that it might never have happened at all. And in the first rush of love, they often wondered at how nearly their paths had crossed during their early teens, when Edward descended occasionally from the remoteness of his squalid family home in the Chiltern Hills to visit Oxford. It was titillating to believe they must have brushed past each other at one of those famous, youthful city events, at St. Giles's Fair in the first week of September, or May

Morning at dawn on the first of the month—a ridiculous and overrated ritual, they both agreed; or while renting a punt at the Cherwell Boathouse—though Edward had only ever done it once; or, later in their teens, during illicit drinking at the Turl. He even thought he may have been bused in with other thirteen-year-old boys to Oxford High, to be thrashed at a general knowledge quiz by girls who were as eerily informed and self-possessed as adults. Perhaps it was another school. Florence had no memory of being on the team, but she confessed it was the sort of thing she liked to do. When they compared their mental and geographical maps of Oxford, they found they had a close match.

Then their childhoods and school years were over, and in 1958 they both chose London—University College for him, for her the Royal College of Music—and naturally they failed to meet. Edward lodged with a widowed aunt in Camden Town and cycled into Bloomsbury each morning. He worked all day, played football at weekends and drank beer with his mates. Until he became embarrassed by it, he had a taste for the occasional brawl outside a pub. His one serious unphysical pastime was listening to music, to the kind of punchy electric blues that turned out to be the true precursor and vital engine of English rock and roll—this music, in his lifelong view, was far superior to the fey three-minute music hall ditties from Liverpool that were to captivate the world in a few years' time. He often left the library in the evenings and walked down Oxford Street to the Hundred Club to listen to John Mayall's Powerhouse Four, or Alexis Korner, or Brian Knight. During his three years as a student, the nights at the club represented the peak of his cultural experience, and for years to come he considered that this was the music that formed his tastes, and even shaped his life.

The few girls he knew—there were not so many at universities in those days—traveled in for lectures from the outer suburbs and left in the late afternoon, apparently under strict parental instruction to be home by six. Without saying so, these girls conveyed the clear impression that they were "keeping themselves" for a future husband. There was no ambiguity—to have sex with any one of these girls, you would have to marry her. A couple of friends, both decent footballers, went down this route, were married in their second year and disappeared from view. One of these unfortunates made a particular impact as a cautionary tale. He got a girl from the university administration office pregnant and was, in his friends' view, "dragged to the altar" and not seen for a year, until he was spotted in Putney High Street, pushing a pram, in those days still a demeaning act for a man.

The Pill was a rumor in the newspapers, a ridiculous promise, another of those tall tales about America. The blues he heard at the Hundred Club suggested to Edward that all around him, just out of sight, men of his age were leading explosive, untiring sex lives, rich with gratifications of every kind. Pop music was bland, still coy on the matter, films were a little more explicit, but in Edward's circle the men had to be content with telling dirty jokes, uneasy sexual boasting and boisterous camaraderie driven by furious drinking, which reduced further their chances of meeting a girl. Social change never proceeds at an even pace. There were rumors that in the English department, and along the road at the School of Oriental and African Studies and down Kingsway at the London School of Economics, men and women in tight black jeans and black polo-neck sweaters had constant easy sex, without having to meet each other's parents. There was even talk of reefers. Edward sometimes took an experimental stroll from the history to the English department, hoping to find evidence of paradise on earth, but the corridors, the notice boards, and even the women looked no different.

Florence was on the other side of town, near the Albert Hall, in a prim hostel for female students where the lights went out at eleven and male visitors were forbidden at any time and the girls were always popping in and out of each other's rooms. Florence practiced five hours a day and went to concerts with her girlfriends. She preferred above all the chamber recitals at the Wigmore Hall, especially the string quartets, and sometimes attended as many as five in a week, lunchtimes as well as evenings. She loved the dark seriousness of the place, the faded, peeling walls backstage, the gleaming woodwork and deep red carpet of the entrance hall, the auditorium like a gilded tunnel, the famous cupola over the stage depicting, so she was told, mankind's hunger for the magnificent abstraction of music, with the Genius of Harmony represented as a ball of eternal fire. She revered the ancient types, who took minutes to emerge from their taxis, the last of the Victorians, hobbling on their canes to their seats, to listen in alert critical silence, sometimes with the tartan rug they had brought draped across their knees. These fossils, with their knobbly shrunken skulls tipped humbly toward the stage, represented to Florence burnished experience and wise judgment, or suggested a musical expertise that arthritic fingers could no longer serve. And there was the simple thrill of knowing that so many famous musicians in the world had performed here and that great careers had begun on this very stage. It was here that she heard the sixteen-year-old cellist Jacqueline du Pré give her debut performance. Florence's own tastes were not unusual, but they were intense. Beethoven's Opus 18 obsessed her for a good while, then his last great quartets. Schumann, Brahms and then, in her last year, the quartets of Frank Bridge, Bartok and Britten. She heard all these composers over a period of three years at the Wigmore Hall.

In her second year she was given a part-time job backstage, making tea for the performers in the spacious green room and crouching by the peephole so that she could open the door as the artistes left the stage. She also turned pages for the pianists in chamber pieces, and one night actually stood at Benjamin Britten's side in a program of songs by Haydn, Frank Bridge and Britten himself. There was a boy treble singing, as well as Peter Pears, who slipped her a ten-shilling note as he and the great composer were leaving. She discovered the practice rooms next door, under the piano showroom, where legendary pianists like John Ogdon and Cherkassky thundered up and down their scales and arpeggios all morning like demented first-year students. The hall became a kind of second home—she felt possessive of every dim and dowdy corner, even of the cold concrete steps that led down to the washrooms. One of her jobs was to tidy the green room, and one afternoon she saw in a wastepaper basket some penciled performance notes discarded by the Amadeus Quartet. The hand was loopy and faint, barely legible, and concerned the opening movement of the Schubert Quartet No. 15. It thrilled her to decipher finally the words, "At B attack!" Florence could not stop herself playing with the idea that she had received an important message, or a vital prompt, and two weeks later, not long after the beginning of her final year, she asked three of the best students at college to join her own quartet.

Only the cellist was a man, but Charles Rodway was of no real romantic interest to her. The men at college, devoted musicians, fiercely ambitious, ignorant of everything beyond their chosen instrument and its repertoire, never much appealed. Whenever one of the girls from the group started going steady with another student, she simply vanished socially, just like Edward's footballer friends. It was as though the young woman had entered a convent. Since it did not seem possible to go out with a boy and still keep up with the old friends, Florence preferred to stick with her hostel group. She liked the banter, the intimacy, the kindness, the way the girls made much of each other's birthdays and fussed around sweetly with kettles, blankets and fruit if you happened to get the flu. Her college years felt like freedom to her.

Edward and Florence's London maps barely overlapped. She knew very little of the pubs of Fitzrovia and Soho, and though she always intended to, she never visited the Reading Room of the British Museum. He knew nothing at all of Wigmore Hall or the tearooms in her quarter, and never once picnicked in Hyde Park or took a boat on the Serpentine. It was exciting for them to discover that they were in Trafalgar Square at the same moment in 1959, along with twenty thousand others, all resolving to ban the bomb.

They did not meet until their London courses were over, when they drifted back to their respective family homes and the stillness of their childhoods to sit out a hot, boring week or two, waiting for their exam results. Later, this was what intrigued them most—how easily the encounter might not have happened. For Edward, this particular day could have passed like most others—a retreat to the end of the narrow garden to sit on a mossy bench in the shade of a giant elm, reading and staying out of his mother's reach. Fifty yards away, her face, pale and indistinct, like one of her watercolors, would be at the kitchen or sitting-room window for twenty minutes at a stretch, watching him steadily. He tried to ignore her, but her gaze was like the touch of her hand on his back or his shoulder. Then he would hear her at the piano upstairs, stumbling through one of her pieces from the Anna Magdalena Notebook, the only piece of classical music he knew of at the time. Half an hour later she might be back at the window, staring at him again. She never came out to speak to him if she saw him with a book. Years ago, when Edward was still a schoolboy, his father had patiently instructed her never to interrupt her son's studies.

That summer, after finals, his interest was in fanatical medieval cults and their wild, psychotic leaders, who regularly proclaimed themselves the Messiah. For the second time in a year he was reading Norman Cohn's *The Pursuit of the Millennium.* Driven by notions of the Apocalypse from the Book of Revelation and the Book of Daniel, convinced the pope was Antichrist and that the end of the world was nearing and only the pure would be saved, rabbles in their thousands would sweep through the German countryside, going from town to town, massacring Jews whenever they could find them, as well as priests and sometimes the rich. Then the authorities would violently suppress the movement, and another sect would spring up elsewhere a few years later. From within the dullness and safety of his existence, Edward read of these recurrent bouts of unreason with horrified fascination, grateful to live in a time when religion had generally faded into insignificance. He was wondering whether to apply for a doctorate, if his degree was good enough. This medieval madness could be his subject.

On strolls through the beech woods, he dreamed of a series of short biographies he would write of semi-obscure figures who lived close to the center of important historical events. The first would be Sir Robert Carey, the man who rode from London to Edinburgh in seventy hours to deliver the news of Elizabeth I's death to her successor, James VI of Scotland. Carey was an interesting figure who usefully wrote his own memoir. He fought against the Spanish Armada, was a superb swordsman and a patron of the Lord Chamberlain's Men. His arduous ride north was supposed to gain him great preferment under the new king, but instead he fell into relative obscurity.

In more realistic moods, Edward thought he should find a proper job, teaching history in a grammar school and making certain he avoided National Service.

If he was not reading, he usually wandered down the lane, along the avenue of limes, to the village of Northend, where Simon Carter, a school friend, lived. But on this particular morning, weary of books and birdsong and country peace, Edward took his rickety childhood bike from the shed, raised the saddle, pumped up the tires and set off with no particular plan. He had a pound note and two half crowns in his pocket and all he wanted was forward movement. At reckless speed, for the brakes barely worked, he flew through a green tunnel, down the steep hill, past Balham's then Stracey's farm, and into the Stonor Valley, and as he hurtled past the iron railings of the park, he made the decision to go on to Henley, another four miles. When he arrived in the town, he headed for the railway station with the vague intention of going to London to look up friends. But the train waiting at the platform was going in the other direction, toward Oxford.

An hour and a half later he was wandering through the city center in the heat of noon, still vaguely bored, and irritated with himself for wasting money and time. This used to be his local capital, the source or promise of nearly all his teenage excitement. But after London it seemed like a toy town, cloying and provincial, ridiculous in its pretensions. When a porter in a trilby scowled at him from the shade of a college entrance, he almost turned back to speak to him. Instead, Edward decided to buy himself a consolatory pint. Going along St. Giles toward the Eagle and Child, he saw a handwritten sign advertising a lunchtime meeting of the local Campaign for Nuclear Disarmament (CND), and hesitated. He did not much like these earnest gatherings, neither the self-dramatizing rhetoric nor the mournful rectitude. Of course the weapons were hideous and should be stopped, but he had never learned anything new at a meeting. Still, he was a paid-up member, he had nothing else to do and he felt a vague pull of obligation. It was his duty to help save the world.

He went along a tiled corridor and entered a dim hall with low painted roof beams and a churchy smell of wood polish and dust through which there rose a low discord of echoing voices. As his eyes adjusted, the first person he saw was Florence, standing by a door talking to a stringy, yellow-faced fellow holding a stack of pamphlets. She wore a white cotton dress that flared out like a party frock, and a narrow blue leather belt tightly fastened around her waist. He thought for a moment she was a nurse—in an abstract, conventional way he found nurses erotic, because—so he liked to fantasize—they already knew everything about his body and its needs. Unlike most girls he stared at in the street or in shops, she did not look away. Her look was quizzical or humorous, and possibly bored and wanting entertainment. It was a strange face, certainly beautiful, but in a sculpted, strong-boned way. In the gloom of the hall the singular quality of light from a high window to her right made her face resemble a carved mask, soulful and tranquil and hard to read. He had not paused as he entered the room. He was walking toward her with no idea of what he would say. In the matter of opening lines, he was reliably inept.

Her gaze was on him as he approached, and when he was near enough she took a pamphlet from her friend's pile and said, "Would you like one? It's all about a hydrogen bomb landing on Oxford."

As he took it from her, her finger trailed,

surely not by accident, across the inside of his wrist. He said, "I can't think of anything I'd rather read."

The fellow with her was looking venomous as he waited for him to move away, but Edward stayed right where he was.

She too was restless at home, a big Victorian villa in the Gothic style just off the Banbury Road, fifteen minutes' walk away. Violet, her mother, marking finals all day in the heat, was intolerant of Florence's regular practice routines—repeated scales and arpeggios, double-stopping exercises, memory tests. "Screeching" was the word Violet used, as in, "Darling, I'm still not finished for today. Could you bear to delay your screeching until after tea?"

It was supposed to be an affectionate joke, but Florence, who was unusually irritable that week, took it as further evidence of her mother's disapproval of her career and hostility to music in general and therefore to Florence herself. She knew she ought to feel sorry for her mother. She was so tone-deaf she was unable to recognize a single tune, even the national anthem, which she could distinguish only by context from "Happy Birthday." She was one of those people who could not say if one note was lower or higher than another. This was no less a disability and misfortune than a clubfoot or a harelip, but after the relative freedoms of Kensington, Florence was finding home life minutely oppressive and could not muster her sympathies. For example, she did not mind making her bed every morning—she had always done so—but she resented being asked at each breakfast whether she had.

As often happened when she had been away, her father aroused in her conflicting emotions. There were times when she found him physically repellent and she could hardly bear the sight of him—his gleaming baldness, his tiny white hands, his restless schemes for improving his business and making even more money. And the high tenor voice, both wheedling and commanding, with its eccentrically distributed stresses. She hated hearing his enthusiastic reports about the boat, the ridiculously named *Sugar Plum*, which he kept down in Poole harbor. It grated on her, his accounts of a new kind of sail, a ship-to-shore radio, a special yacht varnish. He used to take her out with him, and several times, when she was twelve and thirteen, they crossed all the way to Carteret, near Cherbourg. They never talked about those trips. He had never asked her again, and she was glad. But sometimes, in a surge of protective feeling and guilty love, she would come up behind him where he sat and entwine her arms around his neck and kiss the top of his head and nuzzle him, liking his clean scent. She would do all this, then loathe herself for it later.

And her younger sister got on her nerves, with her new Cockney accent and cultivated stupidity at the piano. How were they supposed to do as their father demanded and play a Sousa march for him when Ruth pretended that she could not count four beats in a bar?

As always, Florence was adept at concealing her feelings from her family. It required no effort—she simply left the room, whenever it was possible to do so undemonstratively, and later was glad she had said nothing bitter or wounding to her parents or sister; otherwise she would be awake all night with her guilt. She constantly reminded herself how much she loved her family, trapping herself more effectively into silence. She knew very well that people fell out, even stormily, and then made up. But she did not know how to start—she simply did not have the trick of it, the row that cleared the air, and could never quite believe that hard words could be unsaid or forgotten. Best to keep things simple. She could only blame herself then, when she felt like a character in a newspaper cartoon, with steam hissing from her ears.

And she had other concerns. Should she go for a rear-desk job with a provincial orchestra—she would count herself extremely lucky to get into the Bournemouth Symphony—or should she remain dependent on her parents for another year, on her father really, and work the string quartet up for its first engagement? That would mean lodging in London, and she was reluctant to ask Geoffrey for extra money. The cellist, Charles Rodway, had offered the spare bedroom in his parents' house, but he was a brooding, intense fellow who gave her fixed, meaningful looks over the music stand. Lodging with him, she would be at his mercy. She knew of a full-time job, hers for the asking, with a Palm Court–style trio in a seedy grand hotel south of London. She had no scruples about the kind of music she would have to play—no one would be listening—but some instinct, or mere snobbery, convinced her she could not live in or near Croydon. She persuaded herself that her college results would help her make up her mind, and so, like Edward fifteen miles away in the wooded hills to the east, she passed her days in a form of anteroom, waiting fretfully for her life to begin.

Back from college, transformed from a schoolgirl, mature in ways that no one in the household appeared to notice, Florence was beginning to realize that her parents had rather objectionable political opinions, and here at least she permitted herself open dissent at the dinner table, in arguments that meandered through the long summer evenings. This was release of a kind, but these conversations also inflamed her general impatience. Violet was genuinely interested in her daughter's membership in CND, although it was trying for Florence, having a philosopher for a mother. She was provoked by her mother's calmness or, more accurately, the sadness she affected as she heard her daughter out and then delivered her own opinion. She said that the Soviet Union was a cynical tyranny, a cruel and heartless state responsible for genocide on a scale that even outdid Nazi Germany and for a vast, barely understood network of political prison camps. She went on about show trials, censorship, absence of rule of law. The Soviet Union had trampled on human dignity and basic rights, it was a stifling occupying force in neighboring lands—Violet had Hungarians and Czechs among her academic friends—and it was expansionist by creed and must be opposed, just as Hitler had been. If it could not be opposed, because we did not have the tanks and men to defend the north German plain, then it had to be deterred. A couple of months later she would point to the building of the Berlin Wall and claim complete vindication—the Communist empire was now one giant prison.

Florence knew in her heart that the Soviet

Union, for all its mistakes—clumsiness, inefficiency, defensiveness surely, rather than evil design—was essentially a beneficial force in the world. It was and always had been for liberating the oppressed and standing up to fascism and the ravages of greedy capitalism. The comparison with Nazi Germany disgusted her. She recognized in her mother's opinions a typical pattern of pro-American propaganda. She was disappointed in her mother, and even said so.

And her father had just the sort of opinions you might expect from a businessman. His choice of words could be a little sharpened by half a bottle of wine: Harold Macmillan was a fool to be giving up the empire without a struggle, a bloody fool not to impose wage restraint on the unions, and a pathetic bloody fool for thinking of going cap in hand to the Europeans, begging to join their sinister club. Florence found it harder to contradict Geoffrey. She could never shake off a sense of awkward obligation to him. Among the privileges of her childhood was the keen attention that might have been directed at a brother, a son.

Last summer her father had taken her out regularly after work in his Humber, so that she could have a go at her driving license just after her twenty-first birthday. She failed. Violin lessons from the age of five, with summer courses at a special school, skiing and tennis lessons and flying lessons, which she defiantly refused. And then the journeys: just the two of them, hiking in the Alps, Sierra Nevada and Pyrenees, and the special treats, the one-night business trips to European cities where she and Geoffrey always stayed in the grandest hotels.

When Florence left her house after midday, after an unvoiced argument with her mother over a trifling domestic detail—Violet did not particularly approve of the way her daughter used the washing machine—she said that she was going to post a letter and would not be wanting lunch. She turned south on the Banbury Road and headed toward the city center with a vague ambition of wandering through the covered market and perhaps bumping into an old school friend. Or she might buy a roll there and eat it on Christ Church meadow, in the shade, by the river. When she noticed the sign in St. Giles, the one Edward would see in fifteen minutes, she absentmindedly drifted in. It was her mother who was occupying her thoughts. After spending so much time with her affectionate friends at the student hostel, she noticed, coming home, how physically distant her mother was. She had never kissed or embraced Florence, even when she was small. Violet had barely ever touched her at all. Perhaps it was just as well. She was thin and bony, and Florence was not exactly pining for her caresses. And it was too late to start now.

Within minutes of stepping out of the sunshine into the hall, it was clear to Florence she had made a mistake coming indoors. As her eyes adjusted, she looked about her with the vacant interest she might give the silverware collection in the Ashmolean. Suddenly a North Oxford boy whose name she had forgotten, a gaunt, twenty-two-year-old boy with glasses, came out of the darkness and trapped her. Without preamble, he began to outline for her the consequences of a single hydrogen bomb falling on Oxford. Almost a decade ago, when they were both thirteen, he had invited her to his home in Park Town, only three streets away, to admire a new invention, a television set, the first she had ever seen. On a small, gray, cloudy screen framed by carved mahogany doors, a man in a dinner jacket sat at a desk in what looked like a blizzard. Florence thought it was a ridiculous contraption without a future, but forever after, this boy—John? David? Michael?—seemed to believe she owed him her friendship, and here he was again, still calling in the debt.

His pamphlet, two hundred copies of which were under his arm, set out Oxford's fate. He wanted her to help him distribute them about the town. As he leaned in she felt the scent of his hair cream wrap itself around her face. His papery skin had a jaundiced gleam in the low light, his eyes were reduced by thick lenses to narrow black slits. Florence, incapable of rudeness, settled her face into an attentive grimace. There was something fascinating about tall thin men, the way their bones and Adam's apple lurked so unconcealed beneath the skin, their birdlike faces, their predatory stoop. The crater he was describing would be half a mile across, a hundred feet deep. Because of radioactivity, Oxford would be unapproachable for ten thousand years. It began to sound like a promise of deliverance. But in fact, outside, the glorious city was exploding with the foliage of early summer, the sun was warming the treacle-colored Cotswold stone, Christ Church meadow would be in full splendor. Here in the hall she could see over the young man's narrow shoulder murmuring figures moving about in the gloom, setting out the chairs, and then she saw Edward, coming toward her.

Many weeks later, on another hot day, they took a punt on the Cherwell, upstream to the Vicky Arms, and later drifted back down toward the boathouse. Along the way they parked among a clump of hawthorns and lay on the bank in deep shade, Edward on his back chewing a stalk of grass, Florence with her head resting on his arm. In a break in the conversation they listened to wavelets pattering under the boat and the muffled knock as it swung against its tree-stump mooring. Occasionally a faint breeze brought them the soothing airy sound of traffic on the Banbury Road. A thrush sang intricately, repeating each phrase with care, then gave up in the heat. Edward was working at various temporary jobs, principally as a groundsman for a cricket club. She was giving all her time to the quartet. Their hours together were not always easy to arrange, and all the more precious. This was a snatched Saturday afternoon. They knew that it was one of the last days of full-blown high summer—it was already early September, and the leaves and grasses, though still unambiguously green, had an exhausted air. The conversation had returned again to those moments, by now enriched by a private mythology, when they first set eyes on each other.

In answer to the question Edward had put several minutes before, Florence said at last, "Because you weren't wearing a jacket."

"What then?"

"Um. Loose white shirt, sleeves rolled up to the elbows, tails almost hanging out . . ."

"Nonsense."

"And gray flannel trousers with a mend in the knee, and scruffy plimsolls starting to come out at the toes. And long hair, almost over your ears."

"What else?"

"Because you looked a bit wild, like you'd been in a fight."

"I'd been on my bike in the morning."

She raised herself up on one elbow to get a better view of his face, and they held each other's gaze. It was still a novel and vertiginous experience for them to look for a minute on end into the eyes of another adult, without embarrassment or restraint. It was the closest they came, he thought, to making love. She pulled the grass stem from his mouth.

"You're such a country bumpkin."

"Come on. What else?"

"All right. Because you stopped in the doorway and looked around at everyone as though you owned the place. Proud. No, I mean, bold."

He laughed at this. "But I was annoyed with myself."

"Then you saw me," Florence said. "And you decided to stare me out."

"Not true. You glanced at me and decided I wasn't worth a second look."

She kissed him, not deeply, but teasingly, or so he thought. In these early days he considered there was just a small chance that she was one of those fabled girls from a nice home who would want to go all the way with him, and soon. But surely not outdoors, along this frequented stretch of river.

He drew her closer, until their noses were almost touching and their faces went dark. He said, "So did you think then it was love at first sight?"

His tone was lighthearted and mocking, but she decided to take him seriously. The anxieties she would face were still far off, though occasionally she wondered what it was she was heading toward. A month ago they had told each other they were in love, and that was both a thrill and afterward, for her, a cause of one night of half waking, of vague dread that she had been impetuous and let go of something important, given something away that was not really hers to give. But it was too interesting, too new, too flattering, too deeply comforting to resist, it was a liberation to be in love and say so, and she could only let herself go deeper. Now, on the riverbank in the soporific heat of one of the last days of this summer, she concentrated on that moment when he had paused at the entrance to the meeting room, and on what she had seen and felt when she looked in his direction.

To aid her memory she pulled away and straightened and looked from his face toward the slow muddy green river. Suddenly it was no longer peaceful. Just upstream, drifting their way, was a familiar scene, a ramming battle between two overladen punts locked together at right angles as they rounded a bend at a slew, with the usual shrieks, piratical shouts and splashing. University students being self-consciously wacky, a reminder of how much she longed to be away from this place. Even as schoolgirls, she and her friends had regarded the students as an embarrassment, puerile invaders of their hometown.

She tried to concentrate harder. His clothes had been unusual, but what she noted was the face—a thoughtful, delicate oval, a high forehead, dark eyebrows widely arched, and the stillness of his gaze as it roamed across the gathering and settled on her, as if he were not in the room at all but imagining it, dreaming her up. Memory unhelpfully inserted what she could not yet have heard—the faint country twang in his voice, close to the local Oxford accent, with its hint of West Country.

She turned back to him. "I was curious about you."

But it was even more abstract than that. At the time it did not even occur to her to satisfy her curiosity. She did not think they were about to meet, or that there was anything she should do to make that possible. It was as if her own curiosity had nothing to do with her—she was really the one who was missing from the room. Falling in love was revealing to her just how odd she was, how habitually sealed off in her everyday thoughts. Whenever Edward asked, How do you feel? or, What are you thinking? she always made an awkward answer. Had it taken her this long to discover that she lacked some simple mental trick that everyone else had, a mechanism so ordinary that no one ever mentioned it, an immediate sensual connection to people and events, and to her own needs and desires? All these years she had lived in isolation within herself and, strangely, from herself, never wanting or daring to look back. In the stone-floored echoing hall with the heavy low beams, her problems with Edward were already present in those first few seconds, in their first exchange of looks.

He was born in July 1940, in the week the Battle of Britain began. His father, Lionel, would tell him later that for two months of that summer history held its breath while it decided whether or not German would be Edward's first language. By his tenth birthday he discovered that this was only a manner of speaking—all over occupied France, for example, children had continued to speak French. Turville Heath was less than a hamlet, more a thin scattering of cottages around the woods and common land on a broad ridge above Turville village. By the end of the thirties, the northeastern end of the Chilterns, the London end, thirty miles away, had been invaded by urban sprawl and was already a suburban paradise. But at the southwestern tip, south of Beacon Hill, where one day a motorway torrent of cars and trucks would surge down through a cut in the chalk toward Birmingham, the land was more or less unchanged.

Just near the Mayhews' cottage, down a rutted, steeply banked track through a beech wood, past Spinney Farm, lay the Wormsley Valley, a backwater beauty, a passing author had written, which had been in the hands of one farming family, the Fanes, for centuries. In 1940 the cottage still took its water from a well, from where it was carried to the attic and poured into a tank. It was part of family lore that as the country prepared to face Hitler's invasion, Edward's birth was considered by the local authority to be an emergency, a crisis in hygiene. Men with picks and shovels came, rather elderly men, and mains water was channeled to the house from the Northend road in September of that year, just as the London Blitz was beginning.

Lionel Mayhew was the headmaster of a primary school in Henley. In the early mornings he cycled the five miles to work, and at the end of the day he walked his bike back up the long steep hill to the heath, with homework and papers piled up in a wicker basket on the front handlebars. In 1945, the year the twin girls were born, he bought a secondhand car for eleven pounds in Christmas Common, from the widow of a naval officer lost on the Atlantic convoys. It was still a rare sight along those narrow chalk lanes then, a motor squeezing past the plow horses and carts. But there were many days when petrol rationing forced Lionel back on his bike.

In the early nineteen fifties, his homecoming routines were hardly typical of a professional man. He would take his papers straightaway into the tiny parlor by the front door that he used as his office and set them out carefully. This was the only tidy room in the house, and it was important for him to protect his working life from his domestic environment. Then he checked on the children—in time, Edward, Anne and Harriet all attended the village school in Northend and walked back on their own. He would spend a few minutes alone with Marjorie, and then he would be in the kitchen, preparing the tea and clearing up breakfast.

It was only in this hour, while supper was cooked, that housework was ever achieved. As soon as the children were old enough, they helped out, but ineffectually. Only the exposed parts of the floors not covered in junk were ever swept, and only items needed for the next day—mostly clothes and books—were tidied. The beds were never made, the sheets rarely changed, the handbasin in the cramped, icy bathroom was never cleaned—it was possible to carve your name in the hard gray scum with a fingernail. It was difficult enough to keep up with immediate needs—the coal to be brought in for the kitchen stove, the sitting-room fire to keep going in winter, semi-clean school clothes to be found for the children. Laundry was done on Sunday afternoons, and that required lighting a fire under the copper tub. On rainy days, drying clothes were spread over the furniture throughout the house. Ironing was beyond Lionel—everything was smoothed out with a hand and folded. There were interludes when one of the neighbors acted as home help, but no one stayed for long. The scale of the task was too great, and these local ladies had their own families to organize.

The Mayhews ate their supper at a folding pine table, hemmed in by the close chaos of the kitchen. Washing up was always left for later. After Marjorie had been thanked by everyone for the meal, she wandered off to one of her projects while the children cleared away and then brought their books to the table for homework. Lionel went to his study to mark exercise books, do administration and listen to the wireless news while he smoked a pipe. An hour and a half or so later he would come out to check on their work and get them ready for bed. He always read to them, separate stories for Edward and the girls. They often fell asleep to the sound of him washing the dishes downstairs.

He was a mild man, chunkily built, like a farm laborer, with milky blue eyes and sandy hair and a short military mustache. He was too old to be called up—he was already thirty-eight when Edward was born. Lionel rarely raised his voice or smacked or belted his children the way most fathers did. He expected to be obeyed, and the children, perhaps sensing the burden of his responsibilities, complied. Naturally they took their circumstances for granted, even though they saw often enough the homes of their friends—those kindly, aproned mothers in their fiercely ordered domains. It was never obvious to Edward, Anne and Harriet that they were less fortunate than any of their friends. It was Lionel alone who bore the weight.

Not until he was fourteen did Edward fully understand that there was something wrong with his mother, and he could not remember the time, around his fifth birthday, when she had abruptly changed. Like his sisters, he grew up into the unremarkable fact of her derangement. She was a ghostly figure, a gaunt and gentle sprite with tousled brown hair, who drifted about the house as she drifted through their childhoods, sometimes communicative and even affectionate, at others remote, absorbed in her hobbies and projects. She could be heard at any hour of the day, and even in the middle of the night, fumbling her way through the same simple piano pieces, always faltering in the same places. She was often in the garden pottering about the shapeless bed she had made right in the center of the narrow lawn. Painting, especially watercolors—scenes of distant hills and church spire, framed by foreground trees—contributed much to the general disorder. She never washed a brush, or emptied the greenish water from the jam jars, or put away the paints and rags, or gathered up her various attempts—none of which were ever finished. She would wear her painting smock for days on end, long after a painting bout had subsided. Another activity—it may have been suggested once as a form of occupational therapy—was cutting pictures out of magazines and gluing them into scrapbooks. She liked to move around the house as she worked, and discarded paper clippings were everywhere underfoot, trodden into the dirt of the bare floorboards. Paste brushes hardened in the opened pots where she left them on chairs and window ledges.

Among Marjorie's other interests were bird watching from the sitting-room window, knitting and embroidery, and flower arranging, all pursued with the same dreamy, chaotic intensity. She was mostly silent, though sometimes they heard her murmuring to herself as she carried through a difficult task, "There . . . there . . . there."

It never occurred to Edward to ask himself if she was happy. She certainly had her moments of anxiety, panicky attacks when her breathing came in snatches and her thin arms would rise and fall at her sides and all her attention was suddenly on her children, on a specific need she knew she must immediately address. Edward's fingernails were too long, she must mend a tear in a frock, the twins needed a bath. She would descend among them, fussing ineffectually, scolding, or hugging them to her, kissing their faces or doing all at once, making up for lost time. It almost felt like love, and they yielded to her happily enough. But they knew from experience that the realities of the household were forbidding—the nail scissors and matching thread would not be found, and to heat water for a bath needed hours of preparation. Soon their mother would drift away, back to her own world.

These fits may have been caused by some fragment of her former self trying to assert control, half recognizing the nature of her own condition, dimly recalling a previous existence and suddenly, terrifyingly, glimpsing the scale of her loss. But for most of the time Marjorie kept herself content with the notion, an elaborate fairy tale in fact, that she was a devoted wife and mother, that the house ran smoothly thanks to all her work and that she deserved a little time to herself when her duties were done. And in order to keep the bad moments to a minimum and not alarm that scrap of her former consciousness, Lionel and the children colluded in the make-believe. At the beginning of meals, she might lift her face from contemplating her husband's efforts and say sweetly as she brushed the straggly hair from her face, "I do hope you enjoy this. It's something new I wanted to try."

It was always something old, for Lionel's repertoire was narrow, but no one contradicted her, and ritually, at the end of every meal, the children and their father would thank her. It was a form of make-believe that was comforting for them all. When Marjorie announced that she was making a shopping list for Watlington market, or that she had more sheets to iron than she could begin to count, a parallel world of bright normality appeared within reach of the whole family. But the fantasy could be sustained only if it was not discussed. They grew up inside it, neutrally inhabiting its absurdities because they were never defined.

Somehow they protected her from the friends they brought home, just as they protected their friends from her. The accepted view locally—or this was all they ever heard—was that Mrs. Mayhew was artistic, eccentric and charming, probably a genius. It did not embarrass the children to hear their mother tell them things they knew could not be true. She did not have a busy day ahead, she had not really spent the entire afternoon making blackberry jam. These were not falsehoods, they were expressions of what their mother truly was, and they were bound to protect her—in silence.

It was a memorable few minutes, then, when Edward at the age of fourteen found himself alone with his father in the garden and heard for the first time that his mother was brain-damaged.

The term was an insult, a blasphemous invitation to disloyalty. *Brain-damaged.* Something wrong with her head. If anyone else had said that about his mother, Edward would have been obliged to get in a fight and deliver a thrashing. But even as he listened in hostile silence to this calumny, he felt a burden lifting. Of course it was true, and he could not fight the truth. Straightaway, he could begin to persuade himself that he had always known.

He and his father were standing under the big elm on a hot, moist day in late May. After days of rain, the air was thick with the abundance of early summer—the din of birds and insects, the scent of mown grass lying in rows on the green in front of the cottage, the thrusting, yearning tangle of the garden, almost inseparable from the woodland fringe beyond the picket fence, pollen bringing father and son the season's first taste of hay fever, and on the lawn at their feet, tiles of sunlight and shade rocking together in a light breeze. In these surroundings, Edward was listening to his father, and trying to conjure for himself a bitter winter's day in December 1944, the busy railway platform at Wycombe, and his mother bundled up in her greatcoat, carrying a shopping bag of meager wartime Christmas presents. She was stepping forward to meet the train from Marylebone station that would take her to Princes Risborough, and on to Watlington, where she would be met by Lionel. At home, Edward was being looked after by a neighbor's teenage daughter.

There is a certain kind of confident traveler who likes to open the carriage door just before the train has stopped in order to step out onto the platform with a little running skip. Perhaps by leaving the train before its journey has ended, he asserts his independence—he is no passive lump of freight. Perhaps he invigorates a memory of youthfulness, or is simply in such a hurry that every second matters. The train braked, possibly a little harder than usual, and the door swung out from this traveler's grasp. The heavy metal edge struck Marjorie Mayhew's forehead with sufficient force to fracture her skull and dislocate in an instant her personality, intelligence and memory. Her coma lasted just under a week. The traveler, described by eyewitnesses as a distinguished-looking City gent in his sixties, with bowler, rolled umbrella and newspaper, scuttled away from the scene—the young woman, pregnant with twins, sprawled on the ground among a few scattered toys—and disappeared forever into the streets of Wycombe, with all his guilt intact, or so Lionel said he hoped.

This curious moment in the garden—a turning point in Edward's life—fixed in his mind a particular memory of his father. He held a pipe in his hand, which he did not light until he finished his story. He maintained a purposeful grip, with forefinger curled around the bowl, and the stem poised a foot or so from the corner of his mouth. Because it was Sunday, his face was unshaven—Lionel had no religious beliefs, though he went through the motions at school. He liked to keep this one morning a week for himself. By not shaving on Sunday mornings, which was eccentric for a man in his position, he deliberately excluded himself from any form of public engagement. He wore a creased collarless white shirt, not even smoothed by hand. His manner was careful, somewhat distant—this was a conversation he must have rehearsed in his thoughts. As he spoke, his gaze sometimes moved from his son's face to the house, as though to evoke Marjorie's condition more precisely, or to watch out for the girls. In conclusion, he put his hand on Edward's shoulder, an unusual gesture, and walked him the last few yards to the very end of the garden, where the rickety wooden fence was disappearing beneath the advancing undergrowth. Beyond was a five-acre field, empty of sheep, colonized by buttercups in two wide diverging swaths like roads.

They stood side by side while Lionel lit his pipe at last, and Edward, with the adaptability of his years, continued to make the quiet transition from shock to recognition. Of course, he had always known. He had been maintained in a state of innocence by the absence of a term for her condition. He had never even thought of her as having a condition, and at the same time had always accepted that she was different. The contradiction was now resolved by this simple naming, by the power of words to make the unseen visible. *Brain-damaged.* The term dissolved intimacy, it coolly measured his mother by a public standard that everyone could understand. A sudden space began to open out, not only between Edward and his mother, but also between himself and his immediate circumstances, and he felt his own being, the buried core of it he had never attended to before, come to sudden, hard-edged existence, a glowing pinpoint that he wanted no one else to know about. She was brain-damaged, and he was not. He was not his mother, nor was he his family, and one day he would leave, and would return only as a visitor. He imagined he was a visitor now, keeping his father company after a long absence overseas, gazing out with him across the field at the broad roads of buttercups parting just before the land fell away in a gentle incline toward the woods. It was a lonely sensation he was experimenting with, and he felt guilty about it, but its boldness excited him too.

Lionel appeared to understand the drift of his son's silence. He told Edward that he had been wonderful with his mother, always kind and helpful, and that this conversation changed nothing. It simply recognized that he was old enough to know the facts. At that point the twins came running into the garden, looking for their brother, and Lionel only had time to repeat, "What I've said changes nothing, absolutely nothing," before the girls were noisily among them, and then pulling Edward toward the house to deliver an opinion on something they had made.

But much else was changing for him around this time. He was at Henley grammar school and was beginning to hear from various teachers that he might be "university material." His friend Simon at Northend, and all the other village boys he ran around with, went to the secondary modern, and would soon be leaving to learn a trade or work on a farm before being called up for National Service. Edward hoped his future would be different. Already there was a certain constraint in the air when he was with his friends, on their side as well as his. With homework piling up—for all his mildness, Lionel was a tyrant on this matter—Edward no longer roamed the woods after school with the lads, building camps or traps and provoking the gamekeepers on the Wormsley or Stonor estates. A small town like Henley had its urban pretensions, and he was learning to conceal the fact that he knew the names of butterflies, birds, and the wildflowers growing on the Fane family's land in the intimate valley below the cottage—the bellflower, chicory, scabious, the ten kinds of orchis and hellebores, and the rare summer snowflake. At school such knowledge might mark him out as a yokel.

Learning of his mother's accident that day changed nothing outwardly, but all the tiny shifts and realignments in his life seemed crystallized in this new knowledge. He was attentive and kindly toward her, he continued to help maintain the fiction that she ran the house and that everything she said really was the case, but now he was consciously acting a part, and doing so fortified that newly discovered, tough little core of selfhood. At sixteen he developed a taste for long moody rambles. It helped clear his mind to be out of the house. He often went along Holland Lane, a sunken chalk track overhung with crumbling mossy banks that ran downhill to Turville, and then walked down the Hambledon Valley to the Thames, crossing at Henley into the Berkshire downs. The term "teenager" had not long been invented, and it never occurred to him that the separateness he felt, which was both painful and delicious, could be shared by anyone else.

Without asking or even telling his father, he hitchhiked to London one weekend for a rally in Trafalgar Square against the Suez invasion. While he was there he decided in a moment of elation that he would not apply to Oxford, which was where Lionel and all the teachers wanted him to go. The town was too familiar, insufficiently different from Henley. He was coming here, where people seemed larger and louder and unpredictable and the famous streets carelessly shrugged off their own importance. It was a secret plan he held to—he did not want to generate early opposition. He was also intending to avoid National Service, which Lionel had decided would be good for him. These private schemes refined further his sense of a concealed self, a tight nexus of sensitivity, longing and hard-edged egotism. Unlike some of the boys at school, he did not loathe his home and family. He took for granted the small rooms and their squalor, and he remained unembarrassed by his mother. He was simply impatient for his life, the real story, to start, and the way things were arranged, it could not do so until he had passed his exams. So he worked hard and turned in good essays, especially for his history master. He was amiable enough with his sisters and parents, and he continued to dream of the day when he would leave the cottage at Turville Heath. But in a sense he already had.

THREE

When Florence reached the bedroom, she released Edward's hand and, steadying herself against one of the oak posts that supported the bed's canopy, she dipped first to her right, then to her left, dropping a shoulder prettily each time, in order to remove her shoes. These were going-away shoes she had bought with her mother one quarrelsome rainy afternoon in Debenhams—it was unusual and stressful for Violet to enter a shop. They were of soft pale blue leather, with low heels and a tiny bow at the front, artfully twisted in leather of darker blue. The bride was not hurried in her movements—this was yet another of those delaying tactics that also committed her further. She was aware of her husband's enchanted gaze, but for the moment she did not feel quite so agitated or pressured. Entering the bedroom, she had plunged into an uncomfortable, dreamlike condition that encumbered her like an old-fashioned diving suit in deep water. Her thoughts did not seem her own—they were piped down to her, thoughts instead of oxygen.

And in this condition she had been aware of a stately, simple musical phrase, playing and repeating itself, in the shadowy ungraspable way of auditory memory, following her to the bedside, where it played again as she took a shoe in each hand. The familiar phrase—some might even have called it famous—consisted of four rising notes, which appeared to be posing a tentative question. Because the instrument was a cello rather than her violin, the interrogator was not herself but a detached observer, mildly incredulous, but insistent too, for after a brief silence and a lingering, unconvincing reply from the other instruments, the cello put the question again, in different terms, on a different chord, and then again, and again, and each time received a doubtful answer. There was no set of words she could match to these notes; it was not as if something were being said. The inquiry was without content, as pure as a question mark.

It was the opening of a Mozart quintet, the cause of some dispute between Florence and her friends because playing it had meant drafting in another viola player and the others preferred to avoid complications. But Florence insisted she wanted someone for this piece, and when she invited a girlfriend from her floor at college to join them for a rehearsal and they sight-read it through, naturally the cellist in his vanity fell for it, and soon enough the others came under its spell. Who could not? If the opening phrase posed a difficult question about the cohesion of the Ennismore Quartet—named after the address of the girls' hostel—it was settled by Florence's resolve in the face of opposition, one against three, and her tough-minded sense of her own good taste.

As she crossed the bedroom, still with her back to Edward, still playing for time, and carefully set her shoes down on the floor by the wardrobe, the same four notes reminded her of this other aspect of her nature. The Florence who led her quartet, who coolly imposed her will, would never meekly submit to conventional expectations. She was no lamb to be uncomplainingly knifed. Or penetrated. She would demand of herself what it was exactly she wanted and did not want from her marriage, and she would say so out loud to Edward and expect to discover some form of compromise with him. Surely what each of them desired should not be at the other's expense. The point was to love, and set each other free. Yes, she needed to speak up, the way she did at rehearsals, and she was going to do it now. She even had the beginnings of a proposal she might make. Her lips parted, and she drew breath. Then, at the sound of a floorboard, she turned, and he was coming toward her, smiling, his beautiful face a little pink, and the liberating idea—as if never quite her own—was gone.

Her going-away dress was of a light summer cotton in cornflower blue, a perfect match for her shoes, and discovered only after many pavement hours between Regent Street and Marble Arch, thankfully without her mother. When Edward drew Florence into his embrace, it was not to kiss her, but first to press her body against his, and then to put a hand on her nape and feel for the zip of this dress. His other hand was flat and firm against the small of her back, and he was whispering in her ear, so loudly, so closely that she heard only a roar of warm moist air. But the zip could not be unfastened with one hand alone, at least, not for the first inch or two. You had to hold the top of the dress straight with one hand while pulling down, otherwise the fine material would bunch and snag. She would have reached over her shoulder to help, but her arms were trapped, and besides, it did not seem right, showing him what to do. Above all, she did not wish to hurt his feelings. With a sharp sigh, he tugged harder at the zip, trying to force it, but the point had already been reached when it would move neither down nor up. For the moment she was trapped inside her dress.

"Oh God, Flo. Just keep still, will you."

Obediently, she froze, horrified by the agitation in his voice, automatically certain that it was her fault. It was, after all, her dress, her zip. It might have helped, she thought, to get free and turn her back, and move nearer the window for the light. But that could appear unaffectionate, and the interruption would admit to the scale of the problem. At home she relied on her sister, who was clever with her fingers, despite her abysmal piano playing. Their mother had no patience for small things. Poor Edward—she felt on her shoulders tremors of effort along his arms as he brought both hands into play, and she imagined his thick fingers fumbling between the folds of pinched cloth and obstinate metal. She was sorry for him, and she was a little frightened of him too. To make even a timid suggestion might enrage him further. So she stood patiently, until at last he freed himself from her with a groan and stepped back.

In fact, he was penitent. "I'm really sorry. It's a mess. I'm so bloody clumsy."

"Darling. It happens to me often enough."

They went and sat together on the bed. He smiled to let her know he did not believe her, but appreciated the remark. Here in the bedroom the windows were open wide toward the same view of hotel lawn, woodland and sea. A sudden shift in wind or tide, or perhaps it was the wake of a passing ship, brought the sound of several waves breaking in succession, hard smacks against the shore. Then, just as suddenly, the waves were as before, tinkling and raking softly across the shingle.

She put her arm around his shoulder. "Do you want to know a secret?"

"Yes."

She took his earlobe between forefinger and thumb and gently tugged his head toward her and whispered, "Actually, I'm a little bit scared."

This was not strictly accurate but, thoughtful though she was, she could never have described her array of feelings: a dry physical sensation of tight shrinking, general revulsion at what she might be asked to do, shame at the prospect of disappointing him, and of being revealed as a fraud. She disliked herself, and when she whispered to him, she thought her words hissed in her mouth like those of a stage villain. But it was better to talk of being scared than admit to disgust or shame. She had to do everything she could to begin to lower his expectations.

He was gazing at her, and nothing registered in his expression to show he had heard her. Even in her difficult state, she marveled at his soft brown eyes. Such kindly intelligence and forgiveness. Perhaps if she stared into them and saw nothing else, she might just be able to do anything he asked of her. She would trust him utterly. But this was fantasy.

He said at last, "I think I am too." As he spoke he placed his hand just above her knee, and slid along, under the hem of her dress, and came to rest on her inner thigh, with his thumb just touching her knickers. Her legs were bare and smooth, and brown from sunbathing in the garden and tennis games with old school friends on the Summertown public courts and two long picnics with Edward on the flowery downs above the pretty village of Ewelme, where Chaucer's granddaughter was interred. They continued to look into each other's eyes—in this they were accomplished. Such was her awareness of his touch, the warmth and sticky pressure of his hand against her skin, that she could imagine, she could *see*, precisely his long, curving thumb in the blue gloom under her dress, lying patiently like a siege engine beyond the city walls, the well-trimmed nail just brushing the cream silk puckered in tiny swags along the line of the lacy trim, and touching too—she was certain of this, she felt it clearly—a stray hair curling free.

She was doing all she could to prevent a muscle in her leg from tightening, but it was happening without her, of its own accord, as inevitable and powerful as a sneeze. It was not painful as it clenched and went into mild spasm, this treacherous band of muscle, but she felt it was letting her down, giving the first indication of the extent of her problem. He surely felt the little storm beneath his hand, for his eyes widened minutely, and the tilt of his eyebrows and the soundless parting of his lips suggested that he was impressed, even in awe, as he mistook her turmoil for eagerness.

"Flo . . . ?" He said her name cautiously, on a dip and a rise, as though wanting to steady her or dissuade her from some headlong action. But he was having to hold down a little storm of his own. His breathing was shallow and irregular, and he kept detaching his tongue from his palate with a soft, sticking sound.

It is shaming sometimes, how the body will not, or cannot, lie about emotions. Who, for decorum's sake, has ever slowed his heart, or muted a blush? Her unruly muscle jumped and fluttered like a moth trapped beneath her skin. She had similar trouble sometimes with her eyelid. But perhaps the tumult was subsiding; she could not be sure. It helped her to settle on the basics, and she spelled them out for herself with stupid clarity: his hand was there because he was her husband; she let it stay because she was his wife. Certain of her friends—Greta, Hermione, Lucy especially—would have been naked between the sheets hours ago, and would have consummated this marriage—noisily, joyously—long before the wedding. In their affection and generosity, they even had the impression that this was precisely what she had done. She had never lied to them, but neither had she set them straight. Thinking of her friends, she felt the peculiar unshared flavor of her own existence: she was alone.

Edward's hand did not advance—he may have

been unnerved by what he had unleashed—and instead rocked lightly in place, gently kneading her inner thigh. This may have been why the spasm was fading, but she was no longer paying attention. It must have been accidental, because he could not have known that as his hand palpated her leg, the tip of his thumb pushed against the lone hair that curled out free from under her panties, rocking it back and forth, stirring in the root, along the nerve of the follicle, a mere shadow of a sensation, an almost abstract beginning, as infinitely small as a geometric point that grew to a minuscule smooth-edged speck, and continued to swell. She doubted it, denied it, even as she felt herself sink and inwardly fold in its direction. How could the root of a solitary hair drag her whole body in? To the caressing rhythm of his hand, in steady beats, the single point of feeling spread itself across the surface of her skin, across her belly, and in pulses downward to her perineum. The feeling was not entirely unfamiliar—something between an ache and an itch, but smoother, warmer and somehow emptier, a pleasurable aching emptiness emanating from one rhythmically disturbed follicle, extending in concentric waves across her body and now moving deeper into it.

For the first time, her love for Edward was associated with a definable physical sensation, as irrefutable as vertigo. Before, she had known only a comforting broth of warm emotions, a thick winter blanket of kindness and trust. That had always seemed enough, an achievement in itself. Now here at last were the beginnings of desire, precise and alien, but clearly her own; and beyond, as though suspended above and behind her, just out of sight, was relief that she was just like everyone else. When she was a late-developing fourteen, in despair that all her friends had breasts while she still resembled a giant nine-year-old, she had a similar moment of revelation in front of the mirror the evening she first discerned and probed a novel tight swelling around her nipples. If her mother had not been preparing her Spinoza lecture on the floor below, Florence would have shouted in delight. It was undeniable: she was not a separate subspecies of the human race. In triumph, she belonged among the generality.

She and Edward still held each other's eyes. Talking appeared out of the question. She was half pretending that nothing was happening—that his hand was not under her dress, his thumb was not pushing an outlying pubic hair back and forth, and she was not making a momentous sensory discovery. Behind Edward's head extended a partial view of a distant past—the open door and the dining table by the French window and the debris around their uneaten supper—but she did not let her gaze shift to take it in. Despite the pleasing sensation and her relief, there remained her apprehension, a high wall, not so easily demolished. Nor did she want it to be. For all the novelty, she was not in a state of wild abandonment, nor did she want to be hurried toward one. She wanted to linger in this spacious moment, in these fully clothed conditions, with the soft brown-eyed gaze and the tender caress and the spreading thrill. But she knew that this was impossible, and that, as everyone said, one thing would have to lead to another.

• • •

Edward's face was still unusually pink, his pupils dilated, his lips still parted, his breathing as before: shallow, irregular, rapid. His week of wedding preparation, of crazed restraint, was bearing down hard on his body's young chemistry. She was so precious and vivid before him, and he did not quite know what to do. In the falling light, the blue dress he had failed to remove gleamed darkly against the stretched white counterpane. When he first touched her inner thigh her skin had been surprisingly cool, and for some reason this had excited him intensely. As he looked into her eyes, he had an impression of toppling toward her in constant giddy motion. He felt trapped between the pressure of his excitement and the burden of his ignorance. Beyond the films, the dirty jokes and the wild anecdotes, most of what he knew about women was derived from Florence herself. The perturbation beneath his hand could easily be a telltale sign that anyone could have told him how to recognize and respond to—some kind of precursor to female orgasm, perhaps. Equally, it could be nerves. There was no telling, and he was relieved when it began to subside. He remembered a time, in a vast cornfield outside Ewelme, when he sat at the controls of a combine harvester, having boasted to the farmer that he was competent, and then did not dare touch a single lever. He simply did not know enough. On the one hand, she was the one who had led him to the bedroom, removed her shoes with such abandon, let him place his hand so close. On the other, he knew from long experience how easily an impetuous move could wreck his chances. There again, while his hand remained in place, palpating her thigh, she continued to gaze at him so invitingly—her bold features softened, her eyes narrowing, then opening wide again to find his own, and now her head tilting back—that his caution was surely absurd. This hesitancy was a madness of his own. They were married, for goodness' sake, and she was encouraging him, urging him on, desperate for him to take the lead. But still, he could not escape the memories of those times when he had misread the signs, most spectacularly in the cinema, at the showing of *A Taste of Honey*, when she had leaped out of her seat and into the aisle like a startled gazelle. That single mistake took weeks to repair—it was a disaster he dared not repeat, and he was skeptical that a forty-minute wedding ceremony could make so profound a difference.

The air in the room seemed thin, insubstantial, and it was a conscious effort to breathe. He was troubled by a fit of nervous yawning, which he suppressed with a frown and a flaring of the nostrils—it would not help if she thought he was bored. It pained him tremendously that their wedding night was not simple, when their love was so obvious. He regarded his state of excitement, ignorance and indecision as dangerous because he did not trust himself. He was capable of behaving stupidly, even explosively. He was known to his university friends as one of those quiet types, prone to the occasional violent eruption. According to his father, his very early childhood had been marked by spectacular tantrums. Through his school years and into his time at college he was drawn now and then by the wild freedom of a fistfight. From schoolyard scraps around which savagely chanting kids formed a spectator ring, to a solemn rendezvous in a woodland clearing near the edge of the village, to shameless brawls outside central London pubs, Edward found in fighting a thrilling unpredictability, and discovered a spontaneous, decisive self that eluded him in the rest of his tranquil existence. He never sought out these situations, but when they arose, certain aspects—the taunting, the restraining friends, the squaring up, the sheer outrageousness of his opponent—were irresistible. Something like tunnel vision and deafness descended on him, and then suddenly he was back there again, stepping into a forgotten pleasure, as though emerging into a recurring dream. As in a student drinking bout, the pain came afterward. He was no great pugilist, but he had the useful gift of physical recklessness, and was well placed to raise the stakes. He was also strong.

Florence had never seen this madness in him, and he did not intend to talk to her about it. He had not been in a fight for eighteen months, since January of 1961, in the second term of his final year. It was a one-sided affair, and unusual in that

Edward had some cause, a degree of justice on his side. He was walking along Old Compton Street toward the French Pub in Dean Street with another third-year history student, Harold Mather. It was early evening and they had come straight from the library in Malet Street to meet up with friends. At Edward's grammar school, Mather would have been the perfect victim—he was short, barely five foot five, wore thick glasses over comically squashed features and was maddeningly talkative and clever. At university, however, he flourished, he was a high-status figure. He had an important jazz record collection, he edited a literary magazine, he had a short story accepted, though not yet published, by *Encounter* magazine, he was hilarious in formal student union debates and a good mimic—he did Macmillan, Gaitskell, Kennedy, Khrushchev in fake Russian, as well as various African leaders and comedians like Al Read and Tony Hancock. He could reproduce all the voices and sketches from *Beyond the Fringe* and was reckoned by far the best student in the history group. Edward counted it as progress in his own life, evidence of a new maturity, that he prized his friendship with a man he might once have taken trouble to avoid.

At that time, on a weekday winter's evening, Soho was only just coming to life. The pubs were full, but the clubs were not yet open, and the pavements were uncrowded. It was easy to notice the couple coming toward them along Old Compton Street. They were rockers—he was a big fellow in his mid-twenties, with long sideburns, studded leather jacket, tight jeans and boots, and his plump girlfriend, holding on to his arm, was identically dressed. As they passed, and without breaking stride, the man swung his arm out to deliver a hard, flat-handed smack to the back of Mather's head, which caused him to stagger, and sent his Buddy Holly glasses skidding across the road. It was an act of casual contempt for Mather's height and studious appearance, or for the fact that he looked, and was, Jewish. Perhaps it was intended to impress or amuse the girl. Edward did not stop to think about it. As he strode after the couple, he heard Harold call out something like a "no" or a "don't," but that was just the kind of entreaty he was now deaf to. He was back in that dream. He would have found it difficult to describe his state: his anger had lifted itself and spiraled into a kind of ecstasy. With his right hand he gripped the man's shoulder and spun him around, and, with his left, took him by the throat and pushed him back against a wall. The man's head clunked satisfyingly against a cast-iron drainpipe. Still clenching his throat, Edward hit him in the face, just once, but very hard, with a closed fist. Then he went back to help Mather find his glasses, one lens of which was cracked. They walked on, leaving the fellow sitting on the pavement, both hands covering his face, while his girlfriend fussed over him.

It took Edward some while into the evening to become aware of Harold Mather's lack of gratitude, and then of his silence, or silence toward him, and even longer, a day or two, to realize that his friend not only disapproved, but worse—he was embarrassed. In the pub neither man told their friends the story, and afterward Mather never spoke about the incident to Edward. Rebuke would have been a relief. Without making any great show of it, Mather withdrew from him. Though they saw each other in company, and he was never obviously distant toward Edward, the friendship was never the same. Edward was in agonies when he considered that Mather was actually repelled by his behavior, but he did not have the courage to raise the subject. Besides, Mather made sure they were never alone together. At first Edward believed that his error was to have damaged Mather's pride by witnessing his humiliation, which Edward then compounded by acting as his champion, demonstrating that he was tough while Mather was a vulnerable weakling. Later on, Edward realized that what he had done was simply not cool, and his shame was all the greater. Street fighting did not go with poetry and irony, bebop or history. He was guilty of a lapse of taste. He was not the person he had thought. What he believed was an interesting quirk, a rough virtue, turned out to be a vulgarity. He was a country boy, a provincial idiot who thought a bare-knuckle swipe could impress a friend. It was a mortifying reappraisal. He was making one of the advances typical of early adulthood: the discovery that there were new values by which he preferred to be judged. Since then, Edward had stayed out of fights.

But now, on his wedding night, he did not trust himself. He could not be certain that the tunnel vision and selective deafness would never descend again, enveloping him like a wintry mist on Turville Heath, obscuring his more recent, more sophisticated self. He had been sitting beside Florence, with his hand under her dress, stroking her thigh for more than a minute and a half. His painful craving was building intolerably, and he was frightened by his own savage impatience and the furious words or actions it might provoke, and so end the evening. He loved her, but he wanted to shake her awake, or slap her out of her straight-backed music-stand poise, her North Oxford proprieties, and make her see how really simple it was: here was a boundless sensual freedom, theirs for the taking, even blessed by the vicar—*with my body I thee worship*—a dirty, joyous, bare-limbed freedom, which rose in his imagination like a vast airy cathedral, ruined perhaps, roofless, fan-vaulted to the skies, where they would weightlessly drift upward in a powerful embrace and have each other, drown each other in waves of breathless, mindless ecstasy. It was so simple! Why weren't they up there now, instead of sitting here, bottled up with all the things they did not know how to say or dared not do?

And what stood in their way? Their personalities and pasts, their ignorance and fear, timidity, squeamishness, lack of entitlement or experience or easy manners, then the tail end of a religious prohibition, their Englishness and class, and history itself. Nothing much at all. He removed his hand and drew her to him and kissed her on the lips, with all the restraint he was capable of, holding back his tongue. He eased her back across the bed so that her head was cushioned on his arm. He lay on his side, propped on the elbow of that same arm, looking down at her. The bed squeaked mournfully when they moved, a reminder of other honeymoon couples who had passed through, all surely more adept than they were. He held down a sudden impulse to laugh at the idea of them, a solemn queue stretching out into the corridor, downstairs to reception, back through time. It was important not to think about them; comedy was an erotic poison. He also had to hold off the thought that she might be terrified of him. If he believed that, he could do nothing. She was compliant in his arms, her eyes still fixed on his, her face slack and difficult to read. Her breathing was steady and deep, like a sleeper's. He whispered her name and told her again that he loved her, and she blinked, and parted her lips, perhaps in assent, or even reciprocation. With his free hand he began to remove her knickers. She tensed, but she did not resist, and lifted, or half lifted, her buttocks from the bed. Again, the sad sound of mattress springs or bed frame, like the bleat of a spring lamb. Even with his free arm at full stretch, it was not possible to continue to cushion her head while hooking the knickers past her knees and around her ankles. She helped him by bending her knees. A good sign. He could not face another attempt on the zip of her dress, so for the moment her bra—pale blue silk, so he had glimpsed, with a fine lace trim—must stay in place too. So much for the bare-limbed weightless embrace. But she was beautiful as she was, lying on his arm, her dress rucked up around her thighs, ropes of her tangled hair spread out across the counterpane. A sun queen. They kissed again. He was nauseous with desire and indecision. To get undressed he would have to disturb this promising arrangement of their bodies and risk breaking the spell. A slight change, a combination of tiny factors, little zephyrs of doubt, and she could change her mind. But he firmly believed that to make love—and for the very first time—merely by unzipping his fly was unsensual and gross. And impolite.

After some minutes, he slid from her side and undressed hurriedly over by the window, leaving a precious zone around the bed free of all such banality. He trod on the backs of his shoes to wrench them from his feet, and snatched his socks off with quick jabs of his thumbs. He observed that her eyes were not on him, but straight up, on the sagging canopy above her. In seconds he was naked but for his shirt, tie and wristwatch. Somehow the shirt, partly concealing, partly emphasizing his erection, like a draped public monument, politely acknowledged the code set by her dress. The tie was clearly absurd, and as he went back toward her he yanked it free with one hand while loosening his top button with the other. It was a confident swaggering motion, and for a moment there returned to him an idea of himself he once had, of a rough-hewn but fundamentally decent and capable fellow, and then it faded. The ghost of Harold Mather still troubled him.

Florence chose not to sit up, or even shift her position; she lay on her back, staring up at the biscuit-colored pleated cloth supported on posts that were intended to conjure, she supposed, an old England of stone-chilled castles and courtly love. She concentrated on the fabric's uneven weave, on a green coin-sized stain—how had that got there?—and on a trailing thread that stirred in currents of air. She was trying not to think of the immediate future, or of the past, and she imagined herself clinging to this moment, the precious present, like an unroped climber on a cliff, pressing her face tight against the rock, not daring to move. Cool air traveled pleasantly over her bare legs. She listened to the distant waves, the call of herring gulls, and to the sound of Edward undressing. Here came the past anyway, the indistinct past. It was the smell of the sea that summoned it. She was twelve years old, lying still like this, waiting, shivering in the narrow bunk with polished mahogany sides. Her mind was a blank, she felt she was in disgrace. After a two-day crossing, they were once more in the calm of Carteret harbor, south of Cherbourg. It was late in the evening, and her father was moving about the dim cramped cabin, undressing, like Edward now. She remembered the rustle of clothes, the clink of a belt unfastened or of keys or loose change. Her only task was to keep her eyes closed and think of a tune she liked. Or any tune. She remembered the sweet scent of almost rotten food in the closed air of a boat after a rough trip. She was usually sick many times on the crossing, and of no use to her father as a sailor, and that surely was the source of her shame.

Nor could she avoid contemplating her immediate future. Her hope was that in whatever was to come, she would regain some version of that spreading, pleasurable sensation, that it would grow and overwhelm her and be an anesthetic to her fears, and deliver her from disgrace. It appeared unlikely. The true memory of the feeling, of being inside it, of truly knowing what it was like, had already diminished to a dry historical fact. It had happened once, like the Battle of Hastings. Still, it was her one chance, and so it was precious, like delicate antique crystal, easily dropped, and another good reason not to move.

She felt the bed dip and shake as Edward climbed onto it, and his face, replacing the canopy, filled her view. Obligingly, she lifted her head so that he could slot his arm under it once more as a cushion. He drew her in tight along the length of his body. She had a view into the darkness of his nostrils and of a solitary bent hair in the left, standing like a bowed man before a grotto, trembling with every exhalation. She liked the sharply defined lines of the badge-shaped indentation on the upper lip. To the right of the philtrum was a rosy blemish, a tiny raised pinprick, the beginnings or the fading traces of a spot. Against her hip she felt his erection, broom-stick hard and pulsing, and to her surprise, she did not mind so much. What she did not want, not just yet, was to see it.

To seal their reunion, he lowered his head and they kissed, his tongue barely grazing hers at the tip, and again, she was grateful. Conscious of the silence from the downstairs bar—no radio, no conversation—they whispered their "I love yous." It soothed her to be invoking, however quietly, the unfading formula that bound them, and that surely proved their interests were identical. She wondered if perhaps she might even make it through, and be strong enough to pretend convincingly, and on later, successive occasions whittle her anxieties away through sheer familiarity, until she could honestly find and give pleasure. He need never know, at least not until she told it, from within the warmth of her new confidence, as a funny story—back then, when she was an ignorant girl, miserable in her foolish fears. Even now she did not mind him touching her breasts, when once she would have recoiled. There was hope for her, and at the thought she moved closer against his chest. He had his shirt on, she assumed, because his contraceptives were in the top pocket, easily reached. His hand was traveling the length of her body and was pulling back the hem of her skirt up to her waist. He had always been reticent about the girls he had made love to, but she did not doubt the wealth of his experience. She felt the summery air through the open window tickling her exposed pubic hair. She was already far gone into new territory, too far to come back.

It had never occurred to Florence that the preliminaries of love would take place in dumb show, in such intense and watchful silence. But beyond the obvious three words, what could she herself say that did not sound contrived or foolish? And since he was silent, she thought this must be the convention. She would have preferred it if they had murmured the silly endearments they used when they lay around in her bedroom in North Oxford, fully clothed, wasting the afternoons away. She needed to feel close to him in order to hold down the demon of panic she knew was ready to overwhelm her. She had to know he was with her, on her side, and was not going to use her, that he was her friend and was kindly and tender. Otherwise it could all go wrong, in a very lonely way. She was dependent on him for this assurance, beyond love, and finally could not help herself issuing the inane command, "Tell me something."

One immediate and benign effect was that his hand stopped abruptly, not far from where it was before, inches below her navel. He gazed down at her, lips quivering a little—nerves, perhaps, or a nascent smile, or a thought evolving into words.

To her relief, he caught the prompt and resorted to the familiar form of stupidity. He said solemnly, "You have a lovely face and a beautiful nature, and sexy elbows and ankles, and a clavicle, a putamen and a vibrato all men must adore, but you belong entirely to me and I am very glad and proud."

She said, "Very well, you may kiss my vibrato."

He took her left hand and sucked the ends of her fingers in turn, and put his tongue on the violin player's calluses there. They kissed, and it was in this moment of relative optimism for Florence that she felt his arms tense, and suddenly, in one deft athletic move, he had rolled on top of her, and though his weight was mostly through his elbows and forearms planted on either side of her head, she was pinned down and helpless, and a little breathless beneath his bulk. She felt disappointment that he had not lingered to stroke her pubic area again and set off that strange and spreading thrill. But her immediate preoccupation—an improvement on revulsion or fear—was to keep up appearances, not to let him down or humiliate herself, or seem a poor choice among all the women he had known. She was going to get through this. She would never let him know what a struggle it was, what it cost her, to appear calm. She was without any other desire but to please him and make this night a success, and without any other sensation beyond an awareness of the end of his penis, strangely cool, repeatedly jabbing and bumping into and around her urethra. Her panic and disgust, she thought, were under control, she loved Edward, and all her thoughts were on helping him have what he so dearly wanted and to make him love her all the more. It was in this spirit that she slid her right hand down between his groin and hers. He lifted a little to let her through. She was pleased with herself for remembering that the red manual advised that it was perfectly acceptable for the bride to "guide the man in."

She found his testicles first, and, not at all afraid now, she curled her fingers softly around this extraordinary bristling item she had seen in different forms on dogs and horses, but had never quite believed could fit comfortably on adult humans. Drawing her fingers across its underside, she arrived at the base of his penis, which she held with extreme care, for she had no idea how sensitive or robust it was. She trailed her fingers along its length, noting with interest its silky texture, right to the tip, which she lightly stroked; and then, amazed by her own boldness, she moved back down a little, to take his penis firmly, about halfway along, and pulled it downward, a slight adjustment, until she felt it just touching her labia.

How could she have known what a terrible mistake she was making? Had she pulled on the wrong thing? Had she gripped too tight? He gave out a wail, a complicated series of agonized, rising vowels, the sort of sound she had heard once in a comedy film when a waiter, weaving this way and that, appeared to be about to drop a towering pile of soup plates.

In horror she let go, as Edward, rising up with a bewildered look, his muscular back arching in spasms, emptied himself over her in gouts, in vigorous but diminishing quantities, filling her navel, coating her belly, thighs, and even a portion of her chin and kneecap in tepid, viscous fluid. It was a calamity, and she knew immediately that it was all her fault, that she was inept, ignorant and stupid. She should not have interfered, she should never have believed the manual. If his jugular had burst, it could not have seemed more terrible. How typical, her overconfident meddling in matters of awesome complexity; she should have known well enough that her attitude in rehearsals for the string quartet had no relevance here.

And there was another element, far worse in

its way and quite beyond her control, summoning memories she had long ago decided were not really hers. She had taken pride, only half a minute before, in mastering her feelings and appearing calm. But now she was incapable of repressing her primal disgust, her visceral horror at being doused in fluid, in slime from another body. In seconds it had turned icy on her skin in the sea breeze, and yet, just as she knew it would, it seemed to scald her. Nothing in her nature could have held back her instant cry of revulsion. The feel of it crawling across her skin in thick rivulets, its alien milkiness, its intimate starchy odor, which dragged with it the stench of a shameful secret locked in musty confinement—she could not help herself, she had to be rid of it. As Edward shrank before her, she turned and scrambled to her knees, snatched a pillow from under the bedspread and wiped herself frantically. Even as she did so, she knew how loathsome, how unmannerly her behavior was, how it must add to his misery to see her so desperate to remove this part of himself from her skin. And actually, it was not so easy. It clung to her as she smeared it, and in parts it was already drying to a cracked glaze. She was two selves—the one who flung the pillow down in exasperation, the other who looked on and hated herself for it. It was unbearable that he should watch her, the punishing, hysterical woman he had foolishly married. She could hate him for what he was witnessing now and would never forget. She had to get away from him.

In a frenzy of anger and shame she sprang from the bed. And still, her other watching self appeared to be telling her calmly, but not quite in words, *But this is just what it's like to be mad.* She could not look at him. It was torture to remain in the room with someone who knew her like this. She snatched her shoes from the floor and ran through the sitting room, past the ruin of their meal, and out into the corridor, down the stairs, out through the main entrance, around the side of the hotel and across the mossy lawn. And even when she reached the beach at last, she did not stop running.

FOUR

In the brief year between his first encounter with Florence in St. Giles and their wedding in St. Mary's less than half a mile away, Edward was often an overnight guest at the large Victorian villa off the Banbury Road. Violet Ponting assigned him to what the family called the "small room," on the top floor, chastely remote from Florence's, with a view over a walled garden a hundred yards long and, beyond, the grounds of a college or an old people's home—he never troubled to discover which. The "small room" was larger than any of the bedrooms at the Turville Heath cottage, and possibly larger than its sitting room. One wall was covered in plain white-painted shelves of Loeb editions in Latin and Greek. Edward liked the association with such austere learning, though he knew he fooled no one by leaving out copies of Epictetus or Strabo on the bedside table. Like everywhere else in the house, the walls of his room were exotically painted white—there was not a scrap of wallpaper in the Ponting domain, floral or striped—and the floor was bare, untreated boards. He had the top of the house to himself, with an extensive bathroom on a half-landing, with Victorian windows of colored glass and varnished cork tiles—another novelty.

His bed was wide and unusually hard. In a corner, under the slope of a roof, was a scrubbed deal table with an Anglepoise lamp and a kitchen chair, painted blue. There were no pictures or rugs or ornaments, no chopped-up magazines, or any other remains of hobbies or projects. For the first time in his life he made a partial effort to be tidy, for this was a room like no other he had known, one in which it was possible to have calm, uncluttered thoughts. It was here one brilliant November midnight that Edward wrote a formal letter to Violet and Geoffrey Ponting declaring his ambition to marry their daughter, and did not quite ask their permission so much as confidently expect their approval.

He was not wrong. They appeared delighted, and marked the engagement with a family lunch one Sunday at the Randolph Hotel. Edward knew too little about the world to be surprised by his welcome into the Ponting household. He politely took it as his due, as Florence's steady boyfriend and then fiancé, that when he hitchhiked or took the train from Henley to Oxford, his room was always there for him, that there were always meals at which his opinions about the government and the world situation would be solicited, that he would have the run of the library and the garden with its croquet and marked-out badminton court. He was grateful, but not at all surprised, when his laundry was absorbed into the family's and a tidy ironed pile appeared on the blanket at the end of his bed, courtesy of the cleaning lady, who came every single weekday.

It seemed only proper that Geoffrey Ponting should want to play tennis with him on the grass courts at Summertown. Edward was a mediocre player—he had a decent serve that made use of his height, and he could hit the occasional beefy shot from the baseline. But at the net he was clumsy and stupid, and he could not trust his mutinous backhand, preferring to run around balls to his left. He was a little frightened of his girlfriend's father, worried that Geoffrey Ponting thought he was an intruder, an impostor, a thief intending an assault on his daughter's virginity, and then disappearing—only one part of which was true. As they drove to the courts, Edward also worried about the game—it would be impolite to win, and it would be a complete waste of his host's time if Edward was unable to put up some decent opposition. He need not have troubled himself on either count. Ponting was in another league, a player of fast and accurate strokes, and an astonishing prancing vigor for a fifty-year-old. He took the first set six-one, the second six-love, the third six-one, but what mattered most was his fury whenever Edward managed to snatch a point. As he walked back to his position, the older player would deliver himself a muttered lecture that, as far as Edward could make out from his end, contained threats of violence against the self. In fact, now and then Ponting smacked his right buttock hard with his racket. He did not just want to win, or win easily; he needed every last point. The two games he lost in the first and third sets and his few unforced errors brought him to near screaming point—Oh for *God's* sake, man! Come *on*! Driving back home he was terse, and Edward could at least feel that the dozen points he had won over three sets made for a victory of sorts. If he had won in the conventional manner, he might never have been allowed to see Florence again.

Generally, Geoffrey Ponting, in his nervous, energetic fashion, was affable toward him. If Edward was at the house when he came in from work, around seven o'clock, he would mix them both gin and tonics from his drinks cupboard—tonic and gin in equal measure, and many ice cubes. To Edward, ice in drinks was a novelty. They would sit in the garden and talk politics—mostly, Edward listened to his future father-in-law's views on the decline of British business, demarcation disputes in the trade unions and the folly of granting independence to various African colonies. Even when Ponting was sitting down he did not relax—he balanced himself on the edge of his seat, ready to leap up, and he jigged his knee up and down as he spoke, or wiggled his toes inside his sandals in time to a rhythm in his head. He was far shorter than Edward, but powerfully built, with muscular arms matted with blond hair which he liked to display by wearing short-sleeved shirts, even to work. His baldness too appeared an assertion of power rather than age—the tanned skin was stretched smooth and tight, like filled sails, over the large skull. The face also was large, with small fleshy lips whose resting position was a determined pout, and a button nose, and eyes set wide apart so that in certain lights he resembled a giant fetus.

Florence never seemed to want to join them for these garden chats, and perhaps Ponting did not want her there. As far as Edward could tell, father and daughter rarely spoke, except in company, and then inconsequentially. He thought they were intensely aware of each other, though, and had the impression they exchanged glances when other people were talking, as though sharing a secret criticism. Ponting was always putting his arm around Ruth's shoulders, but he never, in Edward's sight, embraced her big sister. For all that, in conversation, Ponting made many gratifying references to "Florence and you" or "you young ones." He was the one, rather than Violet, who became excited by the news of the engagement and arranged the lunch at the Randolph and proposed half a dozen toasts. It crossed Edward's mind, barely seriously, that he was rather too keen to give his daughter away.

It was around this time that Florence suggested to her father that Edward might be an asset to the firm. Ponting drove him one Saturday morning in his Humber to his factory on the edge of Witney, where scientific instruments filled with transistors were designed and assembled. He did not appear at all troubled, as they passed between the tangled benches, through the homely smell of molten solder, that Edward, reliably stupefied by science and technology, could not think of one interesting question to ask. He revived a little when he met, in a windowless back room, the bald, twenty-nine-year-old sales manager, who had a history degree from Durham and had written his doctoral thesis on medieval monasticism in the northeast of England. Over gin and tonics that evening, Ponting offered Edward a job traveling for the firm, securing new business. He would need to read up on the products and a tiny bit about electronics, and even less about contract law. Edward, who still had no career plans and who could easily imagine himself writing history books on trains and in hotel rooms between meetings, accepted, more in the spirit of politeness than of real interest.

The various household jobs Edward volunteered to do tied him yet more closely to the Pontings. In that summer of 1961 he mowed the various lawns many times—the gardener was away sick—split three cords of logs for the woodstove, and drove the second car, an Austin 35, regularly to the dump with junk from the unused garage, which Violet wanted to convert to an extension library. In this same car—he was never permitted the Humber—he delivered Florence's sister, Ruth, to friends and cousins in Thame, Banbury and Stratford, and then collected her. He chauffeured Violet around, once to a Schopenhauer symposium in Winchester, and on the way she grilled him about his interest in millenarian cults. What part did famine or social change have in providing followers? And with their anti-Semitism and attacks on the Church and the merchants, couldn't the movements be seen as an early form of socialism of the Russian type? And then, also provocatively, wasn't nuclear war the modern equivalent to the Apocalypse of the Book of Revelation, and were we not always bound by our history and our guilty natures to dream of our annihilation?

He answered nervously, conscious that his intellectual mettle was being tested. As he spoke, they were driving through the outskirts of Winchester. At the edge of his vision he saw her take out her compact and powder her pinched white features. He was fascinated by her pale, polelike arms and sharp elbows, and wondered again whether she really could be Florence's mother. But now he was obliged to concentrate, as well as drive. He said he believed the difference between then and now was more important than the similarity. It was the difference between, on the one hand, a lurid and absurd fantasy devised by a post–Iron Age mystic, then embellished by his credulous medieval equivalents, and, on the other, the rational fear of a possible and terrifying event it was in our power to prevent.

In tones of crisp reprimand that effectively closed the conversation, she told him he had not quite understood her. The point was not whether the medieval cultists were wrong about the Book of Revelation and the end of the world. Of course they were wrong, but they passionately believed they were right, and they acted on their convictions. Likewise, he himself sincerely believed that nuclear weapons would destroy the world, and he acted accordingly. It was quite irrelevant that he was wrong, that the truth was that such weapons were keeping the world safe from war. This, after all, was the purpose of deterrence. Surely, as a historian, he had learned that down through the centuries mass delusions had common themes. When Edward grasped that she was likening his support for CND with membership in a millenarian sect, he politely withdrew, and they drove the last half-mile in silence. On another occasion he drove Violet to and from Cheltenham, where she gave a lecture to the sixth form at the Ladies' College on the benefits of an Oxford education.

His own was proceeding at a pace. During that summer he ate for the first time a salad with a lemon and oil dressing and, at breakfast, yogurt—

a glamorous substance he knew only from a James Bond novel. His hard-pressed father's cooking and the pie-and-chips regime of his student days could not have prepared him for the strange vegetables—the aubergines, green and red peppers, courgettes and mangetouts—that came regularly before him. He was surprised, even a little put out, on his first visit when Violet served as a first course a bowl of undercooked peas. He had to overcome an aversion, not to the taste so much as to the reputation of garlic. Ruth giggled for minutes on end, until she had to leave the room, when he called a baguette a croissant. Early on, he made an impression on the Pontings by claiming never to have been abroad, except to Scotland to climb the three Munroes of the Knoydart Peninsula. He encountered for the first time in his life muesli, olives, fresh black pepper, bread without butter, anchovies, undercooked lamb, cheese that was not cheddar, ratatouille, saucisson, bouillabaisse, entire meals without potatoes, and, most challenging of all, a fishy pink paste, tarama salata. Many of these items tasted only faintly repellent, and similar to each other in some indefinable way, but he was determined not to appear unsophisticated. Sometimes, if he ate too fast, he came close to gagging.

Some of the novelties he took to straightaway: freshly ground and filtered coffee, orange juice at breakfast, confit of duck, fresh figs. He was in no position to know what an unusual situation the Pontings' was, a don married to a successful businessman, and Violet, a sometime friend of Elizabeth David, managing a household in the vanguard of a culinary revolution while lecturing to students on monads and the categorical imperative. Edward absorbed these domestic circumstances without acknowledging their exotic opulence. He assumed that this was how Oxford university teachers lived, and he would not be caught out appearing impressed.

In fact, he was entranced, he lived in a dream. During that warm summer, his desire for Florence was inseparable from the setting—the huge white rooms and their dustless wooden floors warmed by sunlight, the cool green air of the tangled garden breathed into the house through open windows, the scented blossoms of North Oxford, the fresh hardback books piled on tables in the library—the new Iris Murdoch (she was Violet's friend), the new Nabokov, the new Angus Wilson—and his first encounter with a stereophonic record player. Florence showed him one morning the exposed, glowing orange valves of an amplifier protruding from an elegant gray box, and the waist-high speakers, and she put on for him at merciless volume Mozart's Haffner Symphony. The opening octave leap seized him with its daring clarity—a whole orchestra suddenly spread before him—and he raised a fist and shouted across the room, careless of who heard, that he loved her. It was the first time he had ever said it, to her or to anyone. She mouthed the words back at him, and laughed with delight that he had at last been moved by a piece of classical music. He crossed the room and tried to dance with her, but the music became scurrying and agitated, and they came to a ragged halt and let it swirl around them as they embraced.

How could he pretend to himself that within his narrow existence these were not extraordinary experiences? He managed not to think about it. By temperament he was not introspective, and moving around her house with a constant erection, or so it seemed, dulled or confined his thoughts somewhat. By the unspoken rules of the house, he was permitted to loll about on her bed during the day while she practiced the violin, as long as the bedroom door was left open. He was supposed to be reading, but all he could do was watch her and love her bare arms, her headband, her straight back, the sweet tilt of her chin as she tucked the instrument under it, the curve of her breasts silhouetted against the window, the way the hem of her cotton skirt swung against her tanned calves with the movement of her bowing, and small muscles in those calves rippling as she shifted and swayed. Now and then, she would sigh over some imagined imperfection of tone or phrasing and repeat a passage over and again. Another indicator of mood was her way of turning the pages on the stand, moving on from a piece with a sudden sharp snap of the wrist, or at other times lingeringly, pleased with herself at last, or anticipating new pleasures. He was stirred, almost impressed, by her obliviousness to him—she had the gift of total concentration, whereas he could pass the entire day in a twilight of boredom and arousal. An hour might go by before she appeared to remember he was there, and though she would turn and smile, she would never join him on the bed—fierce professional ambition, or another household protocol, kept her by her stand.

They took walks over Port Meadow, upstream along the Thames to the Perch or the Trout for a pint. When they were not talking about their feelings—Edward was beginning to find those conversations cloying—they talked of their ambitions. He expanded on the series of short histories of half-forgotten figures who stood for a short while at the side of great men, or had their own brief moment in the sun. He described to her Sir Robert Carey's wild dash north, how he had arrived at James's court with his face bloodied following a fall from his horse and how all his exertions had earned him nothing. After his conversation with Violet, Edward had decided to add one of Norman Cohn's medieval cultists, a flagellant Messiah of the 1360s whose coming was foretold, so he and his followers proclaimed, in the prophecies of Isaiah. Christ was merely his precursor, for he was the Emperor of the Last Days as well as God himself. His self-flagellating followers obeyed him slavishly, and prayed to him. His name was Konrad Schmid, and he was probably burned at the stake by the Inquisition in 1368, after which all his huge following simply melted away. As Edward saw it, each history would be no longer than two hundred pages and would be published, with illustrations, by Penguin Books, and perhaps when the series was complete it could be available in a special boxed set.

Naturally, Florence talked about her plans for the Ennismore Quartet. The week before they had gone to their old college and played Beethoven's second Razumovsky right through for her tutor, and he was obviously excited. He told them straightaway that they had a future and must at all costs hang together and work extremely hard. He said they should focus their repertoire, concentrate on Haydn, Mozart, Beethoven and Schubert and leave Schumann, Brahms and all the twentieth-century composers until later. Florence told Edward that there was no other life she wanted, that she could not bear to waste away the years at a rear desk in some orchestra, assuming she could even get a place. With the quartet, the work was so intense, the demands on concentration so huge when each player was like a soloist, the music so beautiful and rich, that every time they played a piece through, they found something new.

She said all this knowing that classical music meant nothing to him. As far as he was concerned, it was best heard in the background at low volume, a stream of undifferentiated mewling, scraping and tooting generally taken to signify seriousness and maturity and respect for the past, and entirely devoid of interest or excitement. But Florence believed his triumphant shout at the opening of the Haffner Symphony was a breakthrough, and so she invited him to come to London with her and sit in on a rehearsal. He was ready to accept—of course, he wanted to watch her at work, but more important, he was curious to find out whether this cellist, Charles, she had mentioned rather too many times was a rival in any sense. If he was, Edward thought he needed to demonstrate his presence.

Because of a summer lull in bookings, the piano showroom next door to the Wigmore Hall was letting the quartet have a rehearsal room for a nominal fee. Florence and Edward arrived well before the others so that she could give him a tour of the hall. The green room, the tiny changing room, even the auditorium and the cupola could hardly account, he thought, for her reverence for the place. She was so proud of the Wigmore Hall, it was as if she had designed it herself. She led him out onto the stage and asked him to imagine the thrill and terror of stepping out to play before a discerning audience. He could not, though he did not say so. She told him that one day it would happen, she had made up her mind: the Ennismore Quartet would perform here, play beautifully and triumph. He loved her for the solemnity of her promise. He kissed her, and then he jumped down into the auditorium and stood three rows back, dead center, and vowed that whatever happened, he would be here on that day, in this very seat, 9C, and he would lead the applause and the bravos at the end.

When the rehearsal began, Edward sat quietly in a corner of the bare room in a state of profound happiness. He was discovering that being in love was not a steady state, but a matter of fresh surges or waves, and he was experiencing one now. The cellist, clearly disconcerted by Florence's new friend, was a pudding of a fellow with a stammer and a terrible skin condition, and Edward was able to feel sorry for him and generously forgive his slavish fixation on Florence, for he too could not keep his eyes off her. She was in a state of trance-like contentment as she settled down to work with her friends. She put on her headband, and Edward, waiting for the session to begin, fell into a reverie, not only about sex with Florence but marriage, and family, and the daughter they might have. Surely it was a mark of his maturity to contemplate such things. Perhaps it was just a respectable variation of an old dream of being loved by more than one girl. She would have her mother's beauty and seriousness, and lovely straight back, and was sure to play an instrument—the violin, probably, though he did not entirely rule out the electric guitar.

On that particular afternoon Sonia, the viola player from Florence's floor, arrived to work on the Mozart quintet. At last they were ready to begin. There was the briefest tightening silence, which may have been scored by Mozart himself. As soon as they started to play, Edward was struck by the sheer volume, and the muscularity of the sound, and the velvety interleaving of the instruments, and for minutes on end he actually enjoyed the music—until he lost the thread and became bored in a familiar way with the prim agitation and sameness of it all. Then Florence called a halt and quietly gave notes, and there was a general discussion until they began again. This happened several times, and repetition began to reveal to Edward a discernible sweet melody, and various passing entanglements between the players, and daring swoops and leaps that he came to look out for next time around. Later, on the train home, he was able to tell her with complete honesty that he had been moved by the music, and he even hummed bits to her. Florence was so touched, she made another promise—again, that thrilling solemnity that seemed to double the size of her eyes. When the great day came for the Ennismore to make its Wigmore Hall debut, they would play the quintet, and it would be especially for him.

In return, he brought to Oxford from the cottage a selection of records he wanted her to learn to love. She sat dead still and listened patiently, with closed eyes and too much concentration, to Chuck Berry. He thought she might dislike "Roll Over Beethoven," but she found it hilarious. She tried to find something appreciative to say about each song, but she used words like "bouncy" or "merry" or "heartfelt," and he knew she was simply being kind. When he suggested that she did not really "get" rock and roll and there was no reason why she should continue to try, she admitted that what she could not stand was the drumming. When the tunes were so elementary, mostly in simple four-four time, why this relentless thumping and crashing and clattering to keep time? What was the point, when there was already a rhythm guitar, and often a piano? If the musicians needed to hear the beats, why not get a metronome? What if the Ennismore Quartet took on a drummer? He kissed her and told her she was the squarest person in all of Western civilization.

"But you love me," she said.

"*Therefore* I love you."

In early August, when a Turville Heath neighbor fell ill, Edward was offered his part-time job, on a temporary basis, as groundsman at the

Turville cricket club. He was to put in twelve hours a week, and he could do them whenever he wanted. He liked to leave the cottage in the early morning, before even his father was awake, and saunter through the noise of birdsong down the lime-tree avenue to the grounds as if he owned the place. During his first week he prepared the pitch for the local derby, the big game against Stonor. He cut the grass, hauled the roller and helped a carpenter who came up from Hambleden to build and paint a new sightscreen. Whenever he was not working or needed around the house, he headed straight for Oxford, not only because he longed to see Florence, but also because he wanted to forestall the visit she was bound to make to meet his family. He did not know what she and his mother would think of each other, or how Florence would react to the filth and disorder of the cottage. He thought he needed time to prepare both women, but as it turned out, it was not necessary; crossing the grounds one hot early Friday afternoon, he found Florence waiting for him in the shadow of the pavilion. She knew his hours, and had taken an early train and walked from Henley toward the Stonor Valley, with a one-inch-to-the-mile map in her hand and a couple of oranges in a canvas satchel. For half an hour she had been watching him as he marked out the far boundary. Loving him from a distance, she said when they kissed.

That was one of the exquisite moments of their early love, when they went slowly, arm in arm, back up the glorious avenue, walking in the center of the lane to take full possession. Now that it was inevitable, the prospect of her encounter with his mother and the cottage no longer seemed important. The shadows the lime trees cast were so deep they appeared bluish black in the brilliant light, and the heath was thick with fresh grasses and wildflowers. He showed off his knowledge of their country names and even found, by luck, by the roadside, a clump of Chiltern gentians. They picked just one. They saw a yellowhammer, a green finch, and then a sparrowhawk flashed by, cutting a narrow angle around a blackthorn tree. She did not know the names even of common birds like these, but she said she was determined to learn.

She was exultant from the beauty of her walk and the clever route she had chosen, leaving the Stonor Valley to go along the narrow farm track into lonely Bix Bottom, past the ruined ivy-covered church of St. James, up the wooded slopes to the common at Maidensgrove, where she discovered an immense expanse of wildflowers, then through the beech woods to Pishill Bank, where a little brick-and-flint church and its churchyard were poised so beautifully on the side of the hill. As she described each place—and he knew them all so well—he imagined her there, on her own, walking toward him for hours, stopping only to frown at her map. All for him. What a gift! And he had never seen her so happy, or so pretty. She had tied back her hair with a scrap of black velvet, she wore black jeans and plimsolls, and a white shirt, through a button-hole of which she had threaded a rakish dandelion. As they walked toward the cottage she kept tugging on his grass-stained arm for another kiss, though of the lightest sort, and for once he happily, or at least calmly, accepted that they would go no further. After she peeled her remaining orange for them to share along the way, her hand was sticky in his. They were innocently thrilled by her clever surprise, and their lives seemed hilarious and free, and the whole weekend lay before them.

The memory of that stroll from the cricket ground to the cottage taunted Edward now, a year later, on his wedding night, as he rose from the bed in the semidarkness. He was feeling the pull of contrary emotions and needed to hold on to all his best, his kindest thoughts of her, or else he thought he would fold, he would simply give up. There was a liquid heaviness in his legs as he crossed the room to retrieve his underpants from the floor. He put them on, picked up his trousers and stood for a good while with them dangling from his hand as he stared out the window at the wind-shrunken trees, darkened now to a continuous gray-green mass. High up was a smoky half-moon, casting virtually no light. The sound of waves collapsing onto the shore at regular intervals broke in on his thoughts, as though suddenly switched on, and filled him with weariness; the relentless laws and processes of the physical world, of moon and tides, in which he generally took little interest, were not remotely altered by his situation. This overobvious fact was too harsh. How could he get by, alone and unsupported? And how could he go down and face her on the beach, where he guessed she must be? His trousers felt heavy and ridiculous in his hand, these parallel tubes of cloth joined at one end, an arbitrary fashion of recent centuries. Putting them on, it seemed to him, would return him to the social world, to his obligations and to the true measure of his shame. Once dressed, he would have to go and find her. And so he delayed.

Like many vivid memories, his recollection of strolling toward Turville Heath with Florence created a penumbra of oblivion around it. They must have arrived at the cottage to find his mother alone—his father and the girls would have still been at school. Marjorie Mayhew was usually flustered by a strange face, but Edward retained no impression of introducing Florence, or of how she responded to the crammed and squalid rooms, and the stench of drains, always at its worst in summer, that drifted in from the kitchen. He had only snatches of memories of the afternoon, certain views, like old postcards. One was through the smeared, latticed window of the sitting room to the bottom of the garden, where Florence and his mother sat on the bench, each with a pair of scissors and copies of *Life* magazine, chatting as they cut up pages. When they came in from school, the girls must have taken Florence to see a neighbor's newborn donkey, for another view showed all three coming back across the green, arm in arm. A third was of Florence taking a tray of tea out into the garden to his father. Oh yes, he should not doubt it, she was a good person, the best, and that summer all the Mayhews fell in love with Florence. The twins came to Oxford with him and spent the day on the river with Florence and her sister. Marjorie was always asking after Florence, though she could never remember her name, and Lionel Mayhew, in all his worldliness, advised his son to marry "that girl" before she got away.

He conjured these memories of last year, the cottage postcards, the walk under the limes, the Oxford summer, not from a sentimental desire to compound or indulge his sorrow but to dispel it and feel himself in love, and to hold back the advance of an element that initially he did not care to admit, the beginnings of a darkening of mood, a darker reckoning, a trace of poison that even now was branching through his being. Anger. The demon he had kept down earlier when he thought his patience was about to break. How tempting to give in to it, now that he was alone and could let it burn. After such humiliation, his self-respect demanded it. And what harm was there in a mere thought? Better to be done with it now, while he stood here, half naked among the ruins of his wedding night. He was aided in his surrender by the clarity that comes with a sudden absence of desire. With his thoughts no longer softened or blurred by longing, he was capable of registering an insult with forensic objectivity. And what an insult it was, what contempt she showed for him with her cry of revulsion and the fuss with the pillow, what a twist of the scalpel, to run from the room without a word, leaving him with the disgusting taint of shame and all the burden of failure. She had done what she could to make the situation worse, and irretrievable. He was contemptible to her, she wanted to punish him, to leave him alone to contemplate his inadequacies without any thought for her own part. Surely it was the movement of her hand, her fingers, that had brought him on. At the memory of that touch, that sweet sensation, fresh sharp-edged arousal began to distract him, enticing him from these hardening thoughts, tempting him to start forgiving her. But he resisted. He had found his theme, and he pushed on. He sensed there was a weightier matter just ahead, and here it was, he had it at last, he burst into it, like a miner breaking through the sides of a wider tunnel, a gloomy thoroughfare broad enough for his gathering fury.

It stood clear before him, and he was an idiot not to have seen it. For a whole year he had suffered in passive torment, wanting her till he ached, and wanting small things too, pathetic innocent things like a real full kiss, and her touching him and letting him touch her. The promise of marriage was his only relief. And then what pleasures she had denied them both. Even if they could not make love until after they were married, there was no need for such contortions, such agonies of restraint. He had been patient, uncomplaining—a polite fool. Other men would have demanded more, or walked away. And if, at the end of a year of straining to contain himself, he was not able to hold himself back and had failed at the crucial moment, then he refused to take the blame. That was it. He rejected this humiliation, he did not recognize it. It was outrageous of her to cry out in disappointment, to flounce from the room, when the fault was hers. He should accept the fact, she did not like kissing and touching, she did not like their bodies to be close, she had no interest in him. She was unsensual, utterly without desire. She could never feel what he felt. Edward took the next steps with fatal ease: she had known all this—how could she not?—and she had deceived him. She wanted a husband for the sake of respectability, or to please her parents, or because it was what everyone did. Or she thought it was a marvelous game. She did not love him, she could not love in the way that men and women loved, and she knew this and kept it from him. She was dishonest.

It is not easy to pursue such hard truths in bare feet and underpants. He drew his trousers on and groped for his socks and shoes, and thought it through all over again, smoothing out the rough edges and the difficult transitions, the bridging passages that lifted free of his own uncertainties, and so perfected his case, and felt as he did so his anger surge again. It was approaching a pitch, and would be meaningless if it remained unspoken. Everything was about to come clear. She needed to know what he thought and felt—he needed to tell her and show her. He snatched his jacket from a chair and hurried from the room.

FIVE

She watched him coming along the strand, his form at first no more than an indigo stain against the darkening shingle, sometimes appearing motionless, flickering and dissolving at its outlines, and at others suddenly closer, as though moved like a chess piece a few squares toward her. The last glow of daylight lay along the shore, and behind her, away to the east, there were points of light on Portland, and the cloud base reflected dully a yellowish glow of streetlamps from a distant town. She watched him, willing him to go slower, for she was guiltily afraid of him, and was desperate for more time to herself. Whatever conversation they were about to have, she dreaded it. As she understood it, there were no words to name what had happened, there existed no shared language in which two sane adults could describe such events to each other. And to argue about it was even further beyond her imagining. There could be no discussion. She did not want to think about it, and she hoped he felt the same. But what else were they to talk about? Why else were they out here? The matter lay between them, as solid as a geographical feature, a mountain, a headland. Unnameable, unavoidable. And she was ashamed. The aftershock of her own behavior reverberated through her, and even seemed to sound in her ears. That was why she had run so far along the beach, through the heavy shingle in her going-away shoes, to flee the room and all that had happened in it, and to escape herself. She had behaved abominably. *Abominably*. She let the clumsy, sociable word repeat itself in her thoughts several times. It was ultimately a forgiving term—she played tennis abominably, her sister played the piano abominably—and Florence knew that it masked rather than described her behavior.

At the same time, she was aware of his disgrace—when he rose above her, that clenched, bewildered look, the reptilian jerkiness along his spine. But she was trying not to think about it. Did she dare admit that she was a tiny bit relieved that it was not only her, that he too had something wrong with him? How terrible, but how comforting it would be if he suffered from some form of congenital illness, a family curse, the sort of sickness to which only shame and silence attach, the way it did to enuresis, or to cancer, a word she superstitiously never spoke aloud for fear it would infect her mouth—silliness, for sure, which she would never confess to. Then they could feel sorry for each other, bound in love by their separate afflictions. And she did feel sorry for him, but she also felt a little cheated. If he had an unusual condition, why had he not told her, in confidence? But she understood perfectly why he could not. She too had not spoken up. How could he have begun to broach the matter of his own particular deformity, what could have been his opening words? They did not exist. Such a language had yet to be invented.

Even as she elaborately thought this through, she knew very well there was nothing wrong with him. Nothing at all. It was her, only her. She was leaning back against a great fallen tree, probably thrown up onto the beach in a storm, its bark stripped by the power of the waves and the wood smoothed and hardened by saltwater. She was wedged comfortably in the angle of a branch, feeling in the small of her back, through the massive girth of the trunk, the residual warmth of the day. This was how an infant might be, securely nestling in the crook of its mother's arm, though Florence did not believe she could ever have nestled against Violet, whose arms were thin and tense from writing and thinking. When Florence was five there was one particular nanny, fairly plump and motherly, with a musical Scots voice and red raw knuckles, but she had left after some unnamed disgrace.

Florence continued to watch Edward's progress along the beach, certain that he could not see her yet. She could drop down the steep bank and double back along the shore of the Fleet, but even though she feared him, she thought it would be too cruel to run away. Briefly, she saw the outline of his shoulders against a silver streak of water, a current that plumed far out to sea behind him. Now she could hear the sound of his footfalls on the pebbles, which meant that he would hear hers. He would have known to come in this direction because it was what they had decided, their after-dinner plan, a stroll on the famous shingle spit with a bottle of wine. They were going to collect stones along the way and compare their sizes to see if storms really had brought order to the beach.

The memory of that lost pleasure did not make her feel particularly sorrowful now, for it was immediately displaced by an idea, an interrupted thought from earlier in the evening. To love, and set each other free. It was an argument she could make, a daring proposal, she thought, but to anyone else, to Edward, it could sound laughable and idiotic, perhaps even insulting. She never could quite get the full measure of her own ignorance, because in some matters she thought she was rather wise. She needed more time. But he would be with her in seconds and the terrible conversation must begin. It was another of her failings that she had no idea what attitude to take with him, no feelings beyond her dread of what he might say, and of what she would be expected to say in return. She did not know if she should be asking for forgiveness, or expecting an apology. She was not in love, or out of love—she felt nothing. She just wanted to be here alone in the dusk against the bulk of her giant tree.

There appeared to be some kind of parcel in his hand. He stopped a good room's length away, and that in itself seemed to her unfriendly, and she felt antagonistic in return. Why had he come chasing after her so soon?

Indeed, there was exasperation in his voice. "There you are."

She could not bring herself to respond to such an inane remark.

"Did you really need to come this far?"

"Yes."

"It must be two miles back to the hotel."

She surprised herself with the hardness in her voice. "I don't care how far it is. I needed to get out."

He let this go. When he shifted his weight, the stones tinkled under his feet. She saw now that it was his jacket that he carried. It was warm and moist on the beach, warmer than it had been during the day. It bothered her that he thought he had to bring a jacket with him. At least he had not put on his tie! God, how irritable she suddenly felt, when minutes ago she was so ashamed of herself. She was usually so keen to have his good opinion, and now she did not care.

He was preparing to tell her what he had come to say, and he moved a step closer. "Look, this is ridiculous. It was unfair of you to run out like that."

"Was it?"

"In fact, it was bloody unpleasant."

"Oh really? Well, it was bloody unpleasant, what you did."

"Meaning what?"

She had her eyes shut as she said it. "You know exactly what I mean." She would torture herself with the memory of her part in this exchange, but now she added, "It was absolutely revolting."

She imagined she heard him grunt, as though punched in the chest. If only the silence that followed had been a few seconds longer, her guilt might have had time to rise up against her, and she might have added something less unkind.

But Edward came out swinging. "You don't have the faintest idea how to be with a man. If you did, it would never have happened. You've never let me near you. You don't know a thing about any of it, do you? You carry on as if it's *eighteen* sixty-two. You don't even know how to kiss."

She heard herself say smoothly, "I know failure when I see it." But it was not what she meant, this cruelty was not her at all. This was merely the second violin answering the first, a rhetorical parry provoked by the suddenness, the precision of his attack, the sneer she heard in all his repeated "you's." How much accusation was she supposed to bear in one small speech?

If she had hurt him, he gave no sign, though she could barely see his face. Perhaps it was the darkness that had emboldened her. When he spoke again, he did not even raise his voice.

"I am not going to be humiliated by you."

"And I'm not going to be bullied by you."

"I'm not bullying you."

"Yes you are. You always are."

"This is ridiculous. What are you talking about?"

She was not sure, but she knew it was the route she was taking. "You're always pushing me, pushing me, wanting something out of me. We can never just be. We can never just be happy. There's this constant pressure. There's always something more that you want out of me. This endless wheedling."

"Wheedling? I don't understand. I hope you're not talking about money."

She was not. It was far from her thoughts. How preposterous to mention money. How *dare* he. So she said, "Well, all right, now you mention it. It's clearly on your mind."

It was his sarcasm that had goaded her. Or his flippancy. What she was referring to was more fundamental than money, but she did not know how to say it. It was his tongue pushing deeper into her mouth, his hand going further under her skirt or blouse, his hand tugging hers toward his groin, a certain way he had of looking away from her and going silent. It was the brooding expectation of her giving more, and because she didn't, she was a disappointment for slowing everything down. Whatever new frontier she crossed, there was always another waiting for her. Every concession she made increased the demand, and then the disappointment. Even in their happiest moments, there was always the accusing shadow, the barely hidden gloom of his unfulfillment, looming like an alp, a form of perpetual sorrow which had been accepted by them both as her responsibility. She wanted to be in love and be herself. But to be herself, she had to say no all the time. And then she was no longer herself. She had been cast on the side of sickliness, as an opponent of normal life. It irritated her, the way he pursued her so quickly along the beach, when he should have given her time to herself. And what they had here, on the shores of the English Channel, was only a minor theme in the larger pattern. She could already see ahead. They would have this argument, they would make up, or half make up, she would be coaxed back to the room, and then the expectations would be laid on her again. And she would fail again. She could not breathe. Her marriage was eight hours old and each hour was a weight on her, all the heavier because she did not know how to describe these thoughts to him. So money would have to do as the subject—in fact, it did perfectly well, because now he was roused.

He said, "I've never cared about money, yours or anyone's."

She knew this was true, but she said nothing. He had shifted position, so now she saw his outline clearly against the dying glow on the water behind him.

"So keep your money, your father's money, spend it on yourself. Get a new violin. Don't waste it on anything I might use."

His voice was tight. She had offended him deeply, even more than she intended, but for now she did not care, and it helped that she could not see his face. They had never talked about money before. Her father's wedding present was two thousand pounds. She and Edward had talked only vaguely of buying a house with it one day.

He said, "You think I wheedled that job out of you? It was your idea. And I don't want it. Do you understand? I don't want to work for your father. You can tell him I've changed my mind."

"Tell him yourself. He'll be really pleased. He's gone to a lot of trouble for you."

"Right then. I will."

He turned and walked away from her, toward the shoreline, and after a few steps came back, kicking at the shingle with unashamed violence, sending up a spray of small stones, some of which landed near her feet. His anger stirred her own and she suddenly thought she understood their problem: they were too polite, too constrained, too timorous, they went around each other on tiptoes, murmuring, whispering, deferring, agreeing. They barely knew each other, and never could because of the blanket of companionable near-silence that smothered their differences and blinded them as much as it bound them. They had been frightened of ever disagreeing, and now his anger was setting her free. She wanted to hurt him, punish him in order to make herself distinct from him. It was such an unfamiliar impulse in her, toward the thrill of destruction, that she had no resistance against it. Her heart beat hard and she wanted to tell him that she hated him, and she was about to say these harsh and wonderful words that she had never uttered before in her life when he spoke first. He was back to his starting point, and calling on all his dignity to reprimand her.

"Why did you run off? It was wrong of you, and hurtful."

Wrong. Hurtful. How pathetic!

She said, "I've already told you. I had to get out. I couldn't bear it, being with you in there."

"You were wanting to humiliate me."

"Oh, all right then. If that's what you want. I was trying to humiliate you. It's no less than you deserve when you can't even control yourself."

"You're a bitch talking like that."

The word was a starburst in the night sky. Now she could say what she liked.

"If that's what you think, then get away from me. Just clear off, will you. Edward, please go *away*. Don't you understand? I came out here to be alone."

She knew he realized he had gone too far with his word, and now he was trapped with it. As she turned her back on him, she was conscious of playacting, of being tactical in a way she had always despised in her more demonstrative girlfriends. She was tiring of the conversation. Even the best outcome would only return her to more of the same silent maneuverings. Often when she was unhappy, she wondered what it was she would most like to be doing. In this instance, she knew immediately. She saw herself on the London-bound platform of Oxford railway station, nine o'clock in the morning, violin case in her hand, a sheaf of music and a bundle of sharpened pencils in the old canvas school satchel on her shoulder, heading toward a rehearsal with the quartet, toward an encounter with beauty and difficulty, with problems that could actually be resolved by friends working together. Whereas here, with Edward, there was no resolution she could imagine, unless she made her proposal, and now she doubted if she had the courage. How unfree she was, her life entangled with this strange person from a hamlet in the Chiltern Hills who knew the names of wildflowers and crops and all the medieval kings and popes. And how extraordinary it now seemed to her, that she had chosen this situation, this entanglement, for herself.

Her back was still turned. She sensed he had drawn closer, she imagined him right behind her, his hands hanging loosely at his sides, softly clenching and unclenching as he considered the possibility of touching her shoulder. From the solid darkness of the hills, carrying right across the Fleet, came the song of a single bird, convoluted and fluting. By the prettiness of the song and the time of day she would have guessed it to be a nightingale. But did nightingales live by the sea? Did they sing in July? Edward knew, but she was in no mood to ask.

He said in a matter-of-fact way, "I loved you, but you make it so hard."

They were silent as the implications of his tense settled around them. Then she said at last, wonderingly, "You *loved* me?"

He did not correct himself. Perhaps he himself was not so bad a tactician. He said simply, "We could be so free with each other, we could be in paradise. Instead we're in this mess."

The plain truth of this disarmed her, as did the reversion to a more hopeful tense. But the word "mess" brought back to her the vile scene in the bedroom, the tepid substance on her skin drying to a crust that cracked. She was certain she would never let such a thing happen to her again.

She answered neutrally, "Yes."

"Meaning what exactly?"

"It's a mess."

There was a silence, a kind of stalemate of indeterminate length, during which they listened to the waves and, intermittently, the bird, which had moved farther off and whose fainter call was of even greater clarity. Finally, as she expected, he put a hand on her shoulder. The touch was kindly, spreading a warmth along her spine and into the small of her back. She did not know what to think. She disliked herself for the way she was calculating the moment when she should turn around, and she saw herself as he might, as awkward and brittle like her mother, hard to know, making difficulties when they could be at ease in paradise. So she should make things simple. It was her duty, her marital duty.

As she turned, she stepped clear of his touch because she did not want to be kissed, not straightaway. She needed a clear mind to tell him her plan. But they were still close enough for her to make out some part of his features in the poor light. Perhaps at that moment the moon behind her was partly unmasked. She thought he was looking at her in the way he often did—it was a look of wonder—whenever he was about to tell her that she was beautiful. She never really believed him, and it bothered her when he said it because he might want something she could only fail to give. Thrown by this thought, she could not come to her point.

She found herself asking, "Is it a nightingale?"

"It's a blackbird."

"At night?" She could not conceal her disappointment.

"It must be a prime site. The poor fellow's having to work hard." Then he added, "Like me."

Immediately she laughed. It was as if she had partly forgotten him, his true nature, and now he was clearly before her, the man she loved, her old friend, who said unpredictable, endearing things.

But it was uncomfortable laughter, for she was feeling a little mad. She had never known her own feelings, her moods, to dip and swerve so. And now she was about to make a suggestion that from one point of view was entirely sensible, and from another, quite probably—she could not be sure—entirely outrageous. She felt as though she were trying to reinvent existence itself. She was bound to get it wrong.

Prompted by her laughter, he moved closer to her again and tried to take her hand, and again she moved away. It was crucial to be able to think straight. She started her speech as she had rehearsed it in her thoughts, with the all-important declaration.

"You know I love you. Very, very much. And I know you love me. I've never doubted it. I love being with you, and I want to spend my life with you, and you say you feel the same way. It should all be quite simple. But it isn't—we're in a mess, like you said. Even with all this love. I also know that it's completely my fault, and we both know why. It must be pretty obvious to you by now that . . ."

She faltered; he went to speak, but she raised her hand.

"That I'm pretty hopeless, absolutely hopeless at sex. Not only am I no good at it, I don't seem to need it like other people, like you do. It just isn't something that's part of me. I don't like it, I don't like the thought of it. I have no idea why that is, but I think it isn't going to change. Not immediately. At least, I can't imagine it changing. And if I don't say this now, we'll always be struggling with it, and it's going to cause you a lot of unhappiness, and me too."

This time when she paused he remained silent. He was six feet away, now no more than a silhouette, and quite still. She felt fearful, and made herself go on.

"Perhaps I should be psychoanalyzed. Perhaps what I really need to do is kill my mother and marry my father."

The brave little joke she had thought of earlier, to soften her message or make herself sound less unworldly, brought no response from Edward. He remained an unreadable, two-dimensional shape against the sea, utterly still. With an uncertain, fluttering movement, her hand rose to her forehead to brush back an imaginary trailing hair. In her nervousness she began to speak faster, though her words were crisply enunciated. Like a skater on thinning ice, she accelerated to save herself from drowning. She tore through her sentences, as though speed alone would generate sense, as though she could propel him too past contradictions, swing him so fast along the curve of her intention that there could be no objection he could grasp at. Because she did not slur her words, she sounded unfortunately brisk, when in fact she was close to despair.

"I've thought about this carefully, and it's not as stupid as it sounds. I mean, on first hearing. We love each other—that's a given. Neither of us doubts it. We already know how happy we make each other. We're free now to make our own choices, our own lives. Really, no one can tell us how to live. Free agents! And people live in all kinds of ways now, they can live by their own rules and standards without having to ask anyone else for permission. Mummy knows two homosexuals, they live in a flat together, like man and wife. Two men. In Oxford, in Beaumont Street. They're very quiet about it. They both teach at Christ Church. No one bothers them. And we can make our own rules too. It's because I know you love me that I can actually say this. What I mean, it's this—Edward, I love you, and we don't have to be like everyone, I mean, no one, no one at all . . . no one would know what we did or didn't do. We could be together, live together, and if you wanted, really wanted, that's to say, whenever it happened, and of course it would happen, I would understand, more than that, I'd want it, I would because I want you to be happy and free. I'd never be jealous, as long as I knew that you loved me. I would love you and play music, that's all I want to do in life. Honestly. I just want to be with you, look after you, be happy with you, and work with the quartet, and one day play something, something beautiful for you, like the Mozart, at the Wigmore Hall."

She stopped abruptly. She had not meant to talk about her musical ambitions, and she believed it was a mistake.

He made a noise between his teeth, more of a

hiss than a sigh, and when he spoke he made a yelping sound. His indignation was so violent it sounded like triumph. "My God! Florence. Have I got this right? You want me to go with other women! Is that it?"

She said quietly, "Not if you didn't want to."

"You're telling me I could do it with anyone I like but you."

She did not answer.

"Have you actually forgotten that we were married today? We're not two old queers living in secret on Beaumont Street. We're man and wife!"

The lower clouds parted again, and though there was no direct moonlight, a feeble glow, diffused through higher strata, moved along the beach to include the couple standing by the great fallen tree. In his fury, he bent down to pick up a large smooth stone, which he smacked into his right palm and back into his left.

He was close to shouting now. "With my body I thee worship! That's what you promised today. In front of everybody. Don't you realize how disgusting and ridiculous your idea is? And what an insult it is. An insult to me! I mean, I mean"—he struggled for the words—"how *dare* you!"

He took a step toward her, with the hand gripping the stone raised, then he spun around and in his frustration hurled it toward the sea. Even before it landed, just short of the water's edge, he wheeled to face her again. "You tricked me. Actually, you're a fraud. And I know exactly what else you are. Do you know what you are? You're frigid, that's what. Completely frigid. But you thought you needed a husband, and I was the first bloody idiot who came along."

She knew she had not set out to deceive him, but everything else, as soon as he said it, seemed entirely true. Frigid, that terrible word—she understood how it applied to her. She was exactly what the word meant. Her proposal was disgusting—how could she not have seen that before?—and clearly an insult. And worst of all, she had broken her promises, made in public, in a church. As soon as he told her, it all fit perfectly. In her own eyes as well as his, she was worthless.

She had nothing left to say, and she came away

from the protection of the washed-up tree. To set off toward the hotel she had to pass by him, and as she did so she stopped right in front of him and said in little more than a whisper, "I am sorry, Edward. I am most terribly sorry."

She paused a moment, she lingered there, waiting for his reply, then she went on her way.

Her words, their particular archaic construction, would haunt him for a long time to come. He would wake in the night and hear them, or something like their echo, and their yearning, regretful tone, and he would groan at the memory of that moment, of his silence and of the way he angrily turned from her, of how he then stayed out on the beach another hour, savoring the full deliciousness of the injury and wrong and insult she had inflicted on him, elevated by a mawkish sense of himself as being wholesomely and tragically in the right. He walked up and down on the exhausting shingle, hurling stones at the sea and shouting obscenities. Then he slumped by the tree and fell into a daydream of self-pity until he could fire up his rage again. He stood at the water's edge thinking about her, and in his distraction let the waves wash over his shoes. Finally he trudged slowly back along the beach, stopping often to address in his mind a stern impartial judge who understood his case completely. In his misfortune, he felt almost noble.

By the time he reached the hotel, she had packed her overnight case and gone. She left no note in the room. At reception he spoke to the two lads who had served the dinner from the trolley. Though they did not say so, they were clearly surprised that he did not know that there had been a family illness and his wife had been urgently called home. The assistant manager had kindly driven her to Dorchester, where she was hoping to catch the last train and make a late connection to Oxford. As Edward turned to go upstairs to the honeymoon suite, he did not actually see the young men exchange their meaningful glance, but he could imagine it well enough.

He lay awake for the rest of the night on the four-poster bed, fully dressed, still furious. His thoughts chased themselves around in a dance, in a delirium of constant return. To marry him, then deny him, it was monstrous, wanted him to go with other women, perhaps she wanted to watch, it was a humiliation, it was unbelievable, no one would believe it, said she loved him, he hardly ever saw her breasts, tricked him into marriage, didn't even know how to kiss, fooled him, conned him, no one must know, had to remain his shameful secret, that she married him then denied him, it was monstrous . . .

Just before dawn he got up and went through to the sitting room and, standing behind his chair, scraped the solidified gravy from the meat and potatoes on his plate and ate them. After that, he emptied her plate—he did not care whose plate it was. Then he ate all the mints, and then the cheese. He left the hotel as dawn was breaking and drove Violet Ponting's little car along miles of narrow lanes with high hedges, with the smell of fresh dung and mown grass rushing through the open window, until he joined the empty arterial road toward Oxford.

He left the car outside the Pontings' house with the keys in the ignition. Without a glance toward Florence's window, he hurried off through the town with his suitcase to catch an early train. In a daze of exhaustion, he made the long walk from Henley to Turville Heath, taking care to avoid the route she had taken the year before. Why should he walk in her footsteps? Once home, he refused to explain himself to his father. His mother had already forgotten that he was married. The twins pestered him constantly with their questions and clever speculations. He took them to the bottom of the garden and made Harriet and Anne swear, solemnly and separately, hands on hearts, that they would never mention Florence's name again.

A week later he learned from his father that Mrs. Ponting had efficiently arranged the return of all the wedding presents. Between them, Lionel and Violet quietly set in motion a divorce on the grounds of nonconsummation. At his father's prompting, Edward wrote a formal letter to Geoffrey Ponting, chairman of Ponting Electronics, regretting a "change of heart" and, without mentioning Florence, offered an apology, his resignation and a brief farewell.

A year or so later, when his anger had faded, he was still too proud to look her up, or write. He dreaded that Florence might be with someone else and, not hearing from her, he became convinced that she was. Toward the end of that celebrated decade, when his life came under pressure from all the new excitements and freedoms and fashions, as well as from the chaos of numerous love affairs—he became at last reasonably competent—he often thought of her strange proposal, and it no longer seemed quite so ridiculous, and certainly not disgusting or insulting. In the new circumstances of the day, it appeared liberated, and far ahead of its time, innocently generous, an act of self-sacrifice that he had quite failed to understand. Man, what an offer! his friends might have said, though he never spoke of that night to anyone. By then, in the late sixties, he was living in London. Who would have predicted such transformations—the sudden guiltless elevation of sensual pleasure, the uncomplicated willingness of so many beautiful women? Edward wandered through those brief years like a confused and happy child reprieved from a prolonged punishment, not quite able to believe his luck. The series of short history books and all thoughts of serious scholarship were behind him, though there was never any particular point when he made a firm decision about his future. Like poor Sir Robert Carey, he simply fell away from history to live snugly in the present.

He became involved in the administration of various rock festivals, helped start a health-food canteen in Hampstead, worked in a record shop not far from the canal in Camden Town, wrote rock reviews for small magazines, lived through a chaotic, overlapping sequence of lovers, traveled through France with a woman who became his wife for three and a half years and lived with her in Paris. He eventually became a part-owner of the record shop. His life was too busy for newspapers, and besides, for a while his attitude was that no one could honestly trust the "straight" press because everyone knew it was controlled by state, military or financial interests—a view that Edward later disowned.

Even if he had read the papers in those times, he would have been unlikely to turn to the arts pages, to the long, thoughtful reviews of concerts. His precarious interest in classical music had faded entirely in favor of rock and roll. So he never heard about the Ennismore Quartet's triumphant debut at the Wigmore Hall in July 1968. The *Times* critic welcomed the arrival of "fresh blood, youthful passion to the current scene." He praised the "insight, the brooding intensity, the incisiveness of the playing," which suggested "an astonishing musical maturity in players still in their twenties. They commanded with magisterial ease the full panoply of harmonic and dynamic effects and rich contrapuntal writing that typifies Mozart's late style. His D Major Quintet was never so sensitively rendered." At the end of his review he singled out the leader, the first violinist. "Then came a searingly expressive Adagio of consummate beauty and spiritual power. Miss Ponting, in the lilting tenderness of her tone and the lyrical delicacy of her phrasing, played, if I may put it this way, like a woman in love, not only with Mozart, or with music, but with life itself."

And even if Edward had read that review, he could not have known—no one knew but Florence—that as the house lights came up, and as the dazed young players stood to acknowledge the rapturous applause, the first violinist could not help her gaze traveling to the middle of the third row, to seat 9C.

In later years, whenever Edward thought of her and addressed her in his mind, or imagined writing to her or bumping into her in the street, it seemed to him that an explanation of his existence would take up less than a minute, less than half a page. What had he done with himself? He had drifted through, half asleep, inattentive, unambitious, unserious, childless, comfortable. His modest achievements were mostly material. He owned a tiny flat in Camden Town, a share of a two-bedroom cottage in the Auvergne, and two specialist record stores, jazz and rock and roll, precarious ventures slowly being undermined by Internet shopping. He supposed he was considered a decent friend by his friends, and there had been some good times, wild times, especially in the early years. He was godfather to five children, though it was not until their late teens or early twenties that he started to play a role.

In 1976 Edward's mother died, and four years later he moved back to the cottage to take care of his father, who was suffering from rapidly advancing Parkinson's disease. Harriet and Anne were married with children and both lived abroad. By then Edward, at forty, had a failed marriage behind him. He traveled to London three times a week to take care of the shops. His father died at home in 1983 and was buried in Pishill churchyard, alongside his wife. Edward remained in the cottage as a tenant—his sisters were the legal owners now. Initially he used the place as a bolt-hole from Camden Town, and then in the early nineties he moved there to live alone. Physically, Turville Heath, or his corner of it, was not so very different from the place he grew up in. Instead of agricultural laborers or craftsmen for neighbors, there were commuters or owners of second homes, but all were friendly enough. And Edward would never have described himself as unhappy—among his London friends was a woman he was fond of; well into his fifties he played cricket for Turville Park, he was active in a historical society in Henley, and played a part in the restoration of the ancient watercress beds in Ewelme. Two days a month he worked for a trust based in High Wycombe that helped brain-damaged children.

Even in his sixties, a large, stout man with receding white hair and a pink, healthy face, he kept up the long hikes. His daily walk still took in the avenue of limes, and in good weather he would take a circular route to look at the wildflowers on the common at Maidensgrove or the butterflies in the nature reserve in Bix Bottom, returning through the beech woods to Pishill church, where, he thought, he too would one day be buried. Occasionally, he would come to a forking of the paths deep in a beech wood and idly think that this was where she must have paused to consult her map that morning in August, and he would imagine her vividly, only a few feet and forty years away, intent on finding him. Or he would pause by a view over the Stonor Valley and wonder whether this was where she stopped to eat her orange. At last he could admit to himself that he had never met anyone he loved as much, that he had never found anyone, man or woman, who matched her seriousness. Perhaps if he had stayed with her, he would have been more focused and ambitious about his own life, he might have written those history books. It was not his kind of thing at all, but he knew that the Ennismore Quartet was eminent, and was still a revered feature of the classical music scene. He would never attend the concerts, or buy, or even look at, the boxed sets of Beethoven or Schubert. He did not want to see her photograph and discover what the years had wrought, or hear about the details of her life. He preferred to preserve her as she was in his memories, with the dandelion in her buttonhole and the piece of velvet in her hair, the canvas bag across her shoulder, and the beautiful strong-boned face with its wide and artless smile.

When he thought of her, it rather amazed him, that he had let that girl with her violin go. Now, of course, he saw that her self-effacing proposal was quite irrelevant. All she had needed was the certainty of his love, and his reassurance that there was no hurry when a lifetime lay ahead of them. Love and patience—if only he had had them both at once—would surely have seen them both through. And then what unborn children might have had their chances, what young girl with a headband might have become his loved familiar? This is how the entire course of a life can be changed—by doing nothing. On Chesil Beach he could have called out to Florence, he could have gone after her. He did not know, or would not have cared to know, that as she ran away from him, certain in her distress that she was about to lose him, she had never loved him more, or more hopelessly, and that the sound of his voice would have been a deliverance, and she would have turned back. Instead, he stood in cold and righteous silence in the summer's dusk, watching her hurry along the shore, the sound of her difficult progress lost to the breaking of small waves, until she was a blurred, receding point against the immense straight road of shingle gleaming in the pallid light.

The characters in this novel are inventions and bear no resemblance to people living or dead. Edward and Florence's hotel—just over a mile south of Abbotsbury, Dorset, occupying an elevated position in a field behind the beach parking lot—does not exist.

I.M.

A NOTE ABOUT THE AUTHOR

Ian McEwan is the best-selling author of more than ten books, including the novels *Saturday*; *Atonement*, winner of the National Book Critics Circle Award and the W. H. Smith Literary Award; *The Comfort of Strangers* and *Black Dogs*, both shortlisted for the Booker Prize; *Amsterdam*, winner of the Booker Prize; and *The Child in Time*, winner of the Whitbread Award; as well as the story collections *First Love, Last Rites*, winner of the Somerset Maugham Award; and *In Between the Sheets*. He lives in London.

A NOTE ABOUT THE TYPE

This book was set in a digital version of Monotype Walbaum. The original typeface was created by Justus Erich Walbaum (1768–1839) in 1810. Before becoming a punch cutter with his own type foundries in Goslar and Weimar, he was apprenticed to a confectioner where he is said to have taught himself engraving, making his own cookie molds using tools made from sword blades. The letterforms were modeled on the "modern" cuts being made at the time by Giambattista Bodoni and the Didot family.